George A. McLaughlin

Old Wine in New Bottles

George A. McLaughlin

Old Wine in New Bottles

ISBN/EAN: 9783337330040

Printed in Europe, USA, Canada, Australia, Japan

Cover: Foto ©Andreas Hilbeck / pixelio.de

More available books at **www.hansebooks.com**

OLD WINE IN NEW BOTTLES

OR

OLD TRUTHS RESTATED

BY

REV. G. A. McLAUGHLIN

C. J. PETERS & SON, TYPOGRAPHERS,
BOSTON.

PREFACE.

"No man also having drunk old wine desireth new; for he saith, The old is better." So spake Jesus. He often used striking illustrations, in order to make himself clearly understood. We think there can be no misunderstanding of his meaning here. Old wine is better than new. There is a seasoning that age confers upon it. The older it is, the better it becomes. Old wine represents the one eternal, unchanging religion that has been in the world since the days of Abel. It grows better with time; it improves with age in every individual experience, yet it cannot be improved upon by any art, science, invention, or evolution of man. "Anything that is new in religion," said Mr. Wesley, "is not true." God had to prepare the old wine of the kingdom by the various dispensations. The old wine again and again has had to be put in new bottles, but has itself remained the same. No new wine is needed, only new bottles for the old. The bottles have changed their shape, material, and style with the increasing ingenuity of man; but the old wine admits of no substitute. Many have desired new wine because of the new bottles; but while new wine is not adapted to old bottles, old wine adapts itself to either new or old bottles. We have respect and bow with veneration to those gray-headed truths which by their age prove their fitness to remain. We believe in "the survival of the fittest." And the fittest is that old wine of the kingdom that retains its life and fire. It exhilarated Abraham, made glad the heart of Isaiah, lifted Paul above the depression of his environments, and intoxicated the church of the Pentecost. And there has nothing better been found for the modern church. We deprecate the search or desire for anything as a substitute. Make all the new bottles you will, but there is nothing better than the old wine. We like old wine because it has passed the transition period. It is fixed. The church universal must come back to these old tried truths. There is an insidious sentiment that asserts that there are new tonics, new truths, a new salvation; but we must insist upon the use of the old wine. Old wine imparts *new* vigor. The oldest is really the newest in the kingdom of God. Christianity is a life-force in the soul, and every departure from this ends in formalism, ritualism, decay, and death.   There is danger in these days of substituting for the old wine the frothy, erratic, untried mixtures which breed disease and death.

There are but few points of resemblance between the popular conception of a Christian and the teaching on the subject by the Founder of Christianity.   It may seem rash to assert that after nineteen centuries of Christianity, and in an age noted for Bible study, that the definition of Christianity seems hidden from the multitude.   But as strange things as this have been.   The church of the time of Christ knew the letter of the Bible better than the church of to-day ; but they failed to interpret it in such a manner as to recognize him, although he came according to the prophecy of their Scriptures.   It is not rash, therefore, to assert that modern Christianity may have misapprehended the nature of true Christianity, in this day.   If men failed to recognize Him, they may fail to recognize his Spirit to-day.   There is nothing more talked of than Christianity and the Christian life.   Sometimes we have thought that these things are so much talked of, that they are not understood, because so much is taken for granted without definition or explanation.

Although much is said *about* the subject, we have been unable to find any works that even attempt to define the nature of the Christian in a simple, straightforward, and specific manner. There are works of theology *ad infinitum*. But where is the work that shall simply and plainly define the Christian! The object of this little book is to assert that Christianity, in its primary meaning, is a life-force, and that all who are partakers of that life are seeking the highest form of that life. In other words, this book is an attempt to simply and explicitly define "Christianity according to Christ."

CONTENTS.

OLD WINE IN NEW BOTTLES.

CHAPTER I.

NATURE.

"Partakers of the divine nature." — 2 PET. i. 4.

NEARLY everybody has a definition of the Christian. There are almost as many of these definitions as there are individuals. These definitions are often contradictory to each other, hence they cannot all be true. After nineteen centuries of Christianity, there are more conflicting notions of the nature of the Christian life than ever before.

With such a divergence in the definitions, how shall we know that we ourselves are right ? The answer often given is, " Go to the Bible." To be sure ; but most of those who contradict each other base their claims upon the Bible. Our inquiry, then, must lead us farther than the mere quotation of Bible verses. Who is qualified to know just what the Word of God teaches ? One person has one interpretation, and another has another. Who has the true interpretation ?

There are two simple rules which must guide us in our interpretation of the Bible : —

1. *He who would understand the Scripture must him-self be spiritual, or he will fail to get hold of spiritual truth.*   "The natural man receiveth not the things of the Spirit, neither can he know them, for they are spir-itually discerned."   No person, therefore, is competent to be a religious teacher, and hold up before the people the portrait of a Christian, except he has ceased to be a merely natural man, and has become a spiritual man. This will cut off a great many current notions concern-ing the Christian.

2. *The doctrine of a Christian life that is genuine will be proved by its fruits in the individual man and in society.*

For the present we take up the first proposition only. The carnal mind has so beclouded the human reason, that when man undertakes to reason on spiritual mat-ters he is bewildered.

The scholarly Nicodemus knew nothing of the new birth.   Jesus said to him, "Art thou a master in Israel, and knowest not these things?"

At another time Jesus thanked his Father that he had "hid these things from the wise and prudent, and revealed them unto babes."

It does not follow that, because a man is intel-lectual, therefore he understands spiritual things suffi-ciently to give the Bible definition of a Christian.   We believe the Lord inspires spiritual readers of the Bible to understand it, as truly as he inspired holy men to write it.   Many a child on the mount of experience has seen farther along the way to heaven than philoso-phers who stood at the base.   We do not believe it difficult for one who desires to flee the wrath to come, to lay aside his bosom sins, to deny self and take up his cross, to arrive at the true Bible definition of a Christian. Many current definitions have seemed to be simply excuses to keep on in sin. The sinful heart of man sends forth its noxious vapors, that becloud the human reason in its search for spiritual light. Hence the need of revelation.

I. *A Christian is more than an inhabitant of Christendom.*

Geographers have divided the world into four classes, — Christian, Jewish, Mohammedan, and Pagan. All Turks are Mohammedans ; all Americans are Christians. But being born in a Christian land does not make us Christians. A Christian cannot be created by geography, but by God alone. Many an American is a heathen. And many a man in so-called heathendom is a true Christian. This geographical method of making Christians has puzzled honest heathen, and has been a hindrance to the kingdom of Christ. The opium-trade, forced upon China by so-called Christian England, and the rum-traffic, brought to Africa by so-called Christian America, have become great hindrances to Christianity as taught by Christ. Much of the so-called Christianity of to-day is civilized paganism, which sends its barbarism to foreign lands to injure its weaker brethren. A Christianity which can be proved and located only by the map is spurious.

II. *A Christian is more than a churchman.*

God has blessed organized effort in advancing his kingdom. There has been no permanent prosperity except as the truth has been promoted by organization. This has been the divine method. Because God has

so ordained, some have fallen into the error of worship-
ping the church, just as the Israelites worshipped the
brazen serpent, because God had made it a means of
making his blessing available. Because the church
has been a means of grace, some have relied on the
means instead of the grace. Some worship the cross
more than the Jesus who died on it. They have had
their eyes on the channel more than the water of life
that came through the channel. But men may have
their names on the church-roll who have not their
names in the book of life. The chief members of the
church of Jesus' time were the children of the devil.
People are being deceived right at this point to-day.
After a time they get to ground their salvation on
their church relations, and then they go a step farther,
and are unable to see how any one else can be a real
Christian who does not belong to their sect. But Jesus
said, "Other sheep have I that are not of this fold ;
them also I must bring, and there shall be one fold and
one shepherd." A man may belong to the church like
the Pharisees, and like Judas and Dives, and yet make
his bed in hell.

III. *A Christian is not made by ordinances.*

Some have insisted that the ordinance of baptism
saved men. Such people ground their religion upon
the fact that they have been baptized. Water baptism
is the sign of inward baptizing grace. But as people
get formal, they substitute the sign for that which it
represents. As soon might a man expect to obtain
nourishment from the sign "Groceries" over a store
instead of the food which the sign represented, as to
put the water-sign in place of that repentance and faith

which are the Bible conditions of salvation. Water-baptism is not the forerunner nor prerequisite of the Christian life. Baptism is the sequence, and not the condition, of Christian life. It is the outward profession that God has washed away our sins. Simon Magus was baptized with water; but it did not extract from his soul " the gall of bitterness," nor break " the bonds of iniquity " that enthralled him. He was baptized in the most approved manner, and yet Peter declared " thy heart is not right in the sight of God." On the other hand, the thief on the cross went to heaven without water-baptism at all. To baptize a man to whom God has not given a new nature is simply to exchange a dry sinner for a wet one.

IV. *A Christian is not simply a person who accepts Christ as a guide.*

It is one thing to have a good guide. It is quite another thing to have the strength and ability to follow him. Many an Alpine traveller has procured the services of a guide whom he has not had the strength to follow, or the nerve to imitate, as the guide trod the edge of the precipice, or swung himself out over the yawning abyss thousands of feet in depth.

No human being has been able to safely go by the snares and pitfalls of sin as Jesus did, except as he has had the divine power in his soul to assist him. The example of Christ was not given to make us Christians, but for us to follow after we have become Christians. Only the man who has already become a Christian has become empowered to be like Jesus.

V. *To merely lead a moral life is not to be a Christian.*

Many a man who makes no pretensions to a Christian

life lives as good a life naturally as a professing Christian. So that to be a Christian is not only to lead a
moral life, but something besides that. We can have
morality without religion, but we cannot have true religion without morality. We do not move the hands of
a clock in order to make it perform its required work ;
but we wind up the spring, and properly adjust the parts,
and then the hands go right because the inside is right.
A corpse might, perhaps, be galvanized so as to perform movements similar to those of life. But these
movements would not give life. If there be life and
health, there will be the activities of life and health.
Hence the absurdity of the sentiment we sometimes
hear, " I am trying to be a Christian." In such human
striving there is no more prospect of success than for
a corpse to try to be a live man. Only God can make a
Christian by impartation of divine life. No man ever
became a negro or a Caucasian by trying. He must be
born so. Apple-trees are not apple-trees because they
bear apples, but they bear apples because they are
apple-trees. " Men do not gather grapes from thorns,
nor figs from thistles." Men are not Christians because
they do right. But they do right because they are
Christians.

VI. *To be a Christian is more than to be religious.*

Some think they are Christians because they are religious. A man cannot be a decent heathen without being religious. The Pharisees were exceedingly
religious, but were not Christians at all. Many people
confound religion and salvation. But there is a vast
difference between the two. Some are so busied in
the performance of the externals of Christianity as to

fail to get into its inner spiritual sanctuary. They are so busy polishing the shell that they never open it to get the kernel. They grasp the husks, and let the corn slip through their fingers. They spend a great deal of time on the forms to which they are in bondage. The worst of all bondage is religious bondage. Like a horse in a treadmill, they go the weary round, fearful lest they may leave something undone. To them religion is like an insurance policy for the future ; but the assessments are very exacting now, and there is a fear lest they be unable to keep them paid up. The yoke of mere religion is hard. But the yoke of Jesus Christ is easy. The religion of many seems to consist in keeping their denomination alive and supporting the minister. They have joined the church without being joined to the Lord. They have religion, but not salvation.

VII. *To be a Christian is more than to assent to the creed of Christianity.*

Mere intellectual faith can never save. The devils in hell are a great deal more orthodox in their creed than some people who want to be considered Christians. Men of different schools of thought argue and contend, and seek to convert one another to their system of thought, or interpretation of the Bible, who never have felt the power of true Christianity. Others seek to convert infidels to their faith, who themselves know nothing more of the power of Christ experimentally than the infidel whose views they seek to change. Others contend against the attacks of science upon the Bible who are experimentally as Christless as the scientists themselves. A man may be a Christian in creed and an atheist in his heart.

VIII. *Natural generation cannot make us Christians.*

A certain class of people have much to say about the "Fatherhood of God," and that we are all the dear children of God. This is misleading. Man lost the image of God — spiritual life — when he fell. Paul says to the Ephesians that "by nature we were the children of wrath, even as others." Man is "dead in trespasses and sins" by nature. When Adam sinned he died. Spiritual life left him. Our Universalist friends prate much about the title in the Lord's Prayer — "Our Father." But they forget that it was given to those who were already disciples, saved through the ministry of John the Baptist. We are told by Paul that to be saved is to be "translated out of the kingdom of darkness into the kingdom of God's dear Son." This being true, natural birth can never make us Christians. "The first man is of the earth, earthy;" and so will be his descendants, partaking of his nature. "The second man is the Lord from heaven;" and his "seed," — Christians, — which he should "see and be satisfied," partake of his nature — the heavenly. Jesus forever settled this question, and pointed out the distinction to Nicodemus, when he said "that which is born of the flesh is flesh, and that which is born of the Spirit is spirit." Therefore the command is binding upon every son and daughter of Adam. "Ye must be born again." "*Which were born not of blood,* nor of the will of the flesh, nor of the will of man, but of God." Thus forever crumbles the corner-stone of Universalism.

2. Having treated the definition of the Christian negatively, we now turn to the positive side of the defi-

nition. *A Christian is a person who has become a partaker of the divine nature.* Some years ago a religious newspaper contained a symposium on this question : " What is a Christian ? " Nearly every one who answered defined a Christian by what he does. Scarcely a writer gave a definition of the nature of a Christian. It will be seen at once that this is a very unsatisfactory as well as inexact and unscientific method. It defines nothing. If we were to define a horse as an animal that eats and walks, it would be considered, not only childish, but a waste of words that defined nothing. Natural history divides all creation into different kingdoms, genera, species, etc., and defines each according to the family or order to which it belongs.

In precisely the same way must we define a Christian. He belongs to the spiritual kingdom of God's creation." He is " a new creation."   He is a member of the family of God, a "partaker of the divine nature," "a child of God," " an heir of God," a brother of Jesus Christ, " of whom the whole family in heaven and earth is named." His " citizenship is in heaven;" just now he is passing through a world to which he does not belong. The difference between him and the world about him is that he has been " translated out of the kingdom of darkness into the kingdom of God's dear Son."   In his heart is "shed abroad the love of God."   He "who commanded the light to shine out of darkness hath shined into our hearts, to reveal the knowledge of God in the face of Jesus Christ." Jesus Christ was the first Christian. We are to be like him in spirit. The followers of Satan are like their master. They have the same spirit. The followers of Jesus have the same spirit as he — the

Holy Spirit. "If any man have not the spirit of Christ, he is none of his."

Matthew Arnold says that religion is but morality touched with emotion. When he said that, he no doubt described the religion of many; but his definition shows that he has had no experience in the Christian religion, for that is *a life* — the life of God in the soul. It is a supernatural life, *now* possessed. "He that believeth on the Son *hath* everlasting life."

Those who define religion as simply in the doing instead of the *being*, assert that this is not only mysterious, but a superstition. They sneer at exhibitions of emotion or activity that spring from religious life. Paul, however, who had this experience, declares that it is "the mystery among the Gentiles, which is Christ in you."

Festus said Paul was beside himself. And so do inexperienced men still declare when it is insisted that a true Christian is one who has become a partaker of the nature of Christ.

The fallacy of such sentiments as "Live your religion" is at once manifest as a superfluous precept; for we cannot help living all we have, and we cannot live any more life than we have. But many are endeavoring to live more than they have, and are having a painful, discouraging time of it. Another absurd sentiment is, that "we have all the religion we live for," which means nothing. Just as truly might it be said that a sick man has all the life he lives for, which is really to say nothing. We have all the salvation we trust God for, but not all the religion we live for, because we do not become alive by living for life. This is an empty repetition of words, but it expresses the mystified ideas of many religionists of to-day. They are striving, trying, evolving, endeavoring to fix up the old carnal nature; seeking by evolution, growth, development, etc., to "get religion." One minute of faith will bring spiritual life which amounts to more than ten thousand years of ecclesiastical rites and human works and striving.

In the first part of this chapter we referred to the test of doctrine as given by Jesus, "By their fruits shall ye know them." This is the infallible test of the definition of a Christian. Our definition of the Christian given above must be scriptural, and it must bear the test of its fruitage as seen in society or it is not genuine. *The doctrine of spiritual life in man as essential to being a real Christian has proved itself true in history by its fruits.* The Wesleyan Reformation by its fruits forever settled the question of the spiritual nature of a Christian.

Under contrary teaching, such as baptismal regeneration, salvation by works, ordinances, etc., the church had lost its hold upon society. The more men preached salvation by works, the more society degenerated from good works, until anarchy seemed almost to reign, and it seemed as if England was about to be ruined by the rising tide of wickedness. At this juncture John and Charles Wesley were raised up to preach a spiritual religion that warmed and purified the heart, turned men from sin, and made them "partakers of the divine nature." This purified society, and saved England from destruction. And those churches who to-day are turning men from their sins, reforming the erring, and lifting up the fallen, are essentially preaching the same divine Christ as one who sheds abroad his love in the heart.

These are facts. No other doctrine of the nature of the Christian life has ever borne the fruitage of the Wesleyan doctrine and interpretation of the Christian life.

In accepting this definition of a Christian, we believe it correct because the fruitage is in harmony with the plain teachings of Jesus; namely, that true religion begins in the heart and works outwardly, while all false systems have begun on the outside, and have attempted in vain to work their way into men's hearts. To test an ism or doctrinal system of religion, notice where it begins. If it begins in ceremonies, rites, and outward performances, it begins in the wrong place, and does not make Christians according to the teachings of Jesus Christ. His religion begins in the heart. If it does not begin there, then the unsaved world has as good a religion as the church; for they can perform the externals as well as the best people.

CHAPTER II.

REQUIREMENTS.

"Repentance toward God and faith toward our Lord Jesus Christ."

ACTS XX. 21.

WHAT are the requirements in order to the obtainment of spiritual life, — to become a Christian? who are candidates for the reception of this life of God in the soul? how shall we make our "calling and election sure"? Those who are not sound in their definition of a Christian are usually as far out of the way in their views of the necessary conditions of becoming a Christian. This is quite natural; for when one has a wrong place in view, he takes the wrong path.

No man can become a Christian without taking the two steps required by Jesus Christ. Sin is the same to-day as in the days of Jesus; and the conditions to becoming a Christian, and thus escaping the curse of sin, have never changed. This book is written to show the points at which men have switched off, and failed to come up to the original requirements as given by Jesus Christ. He laid down most rigid terms for those who would become Christians. What would he say, if on earth to-day, at the modern methods of getting men into the church, who never pretend to forsake their sins, and even assert that we cannot be kept from committing sin? The two plain, simple steps to a Christian life are *Repentance* and *Faith*.

I. *Repentance.*

We shall define it negatively. There are certain accompaniments to repentance that are sometimes mistaken for it.

1. *Repentance is not mere sorrow for sin.* — Sorrow to a greater or less degree accompanies repentance. There are men in the penitentiary sorry that they committed the crime that sent them there. But many of them are not penitent, and return to their old life. Pharaoh was sorry at the plagues sent upon him. But he was not a penitent. The prodigal might have wept his life away ; but, had he remained among the harlots and swine, he would not have been a penitent. Although sorrow accompanies repentance, yet people are sometimes sorry for sin who do not exercise repentance toward God.

2. *Repentance is more than a change of mind.* — The word *repentance* is sometimes used, to be sure, in the sense of a change of mind ; but evangelical repentance means more than that. A certain man was sceptical. He had refused to admit the claims of Christ because of a certain objection. He was taken very ill ; and the attending physician told him that he had better prepare at once to meet his God, as he could not recover. His reply was, that he did not believe in the religion of Christ ; at the same time he stated his lifelong objection. The physician, possessed of superior knowledge of the same subject, in a short time cleared away his objection. He did it so thoroughly that the sick man was compelled to acknowledge it. But when urged to repent and accept Christ, he refused, saying " I have made a mistake." He changed his views, but did not

repent of his sins.   Change of views or belief is not repentance.

3. *Acknowledgment of our sins is not repentance.* — Many love to confess their sins in a certain way, who object to having any one else so regard them.   They think it a mark of humility.   We knew of a woman whose reputation was unsavory, who said in a religious meeting that she sinned every day; but, apparently thinking of what was being said of her, she exclaimed, " But if any one says anything against my character, it is a dastardly lie."   Pharaoh said after every one of the ten plagues, " I have sinned ; " but he never repented. King Saul and Balaam said the same thing, but it did not result in repentance.   Many people seem to think that to acknowledge sin gives a kind of license to continue in it.   We sometimes hear it said, " I know it is not right, but I shall do it."

4. *Repentance is the abandonment of sin.* — The Bible command is, " Let the wicked forsake his way ;" "Cease to do evil ;" " Break off your sins by righteousness " — not taper them off, but stop at once.   Hence there is no such thing as a gradual repentance.   There is no such thing in true repentance as leaving off one sin at a time.   Some have defined repentance as turning about. But it is more.   It is *going* to God after we have turned about.   This is repentance *toward* God, of which Paul speaks.   It is the prodigal returning home.   Repentance is accompanied by sorrow for the past, — regret that we have ever sinned.   This regret is so keen that the subject is anxious to make the past as near right as possible.   So it leads to restitution where we have it in our power to restore, or make right where we have in-

jured God or man.   This is the reason that repentance
is so distasteful to many.   It means a great deal.   It
would beggar some people.   But better be Lazarus, a
beggar here, than the rich man in hell.   It leads to
confession when we have injured the feelings or character of others.   A great many people have been serious in religion up to this point; and here they stuck
fast, and lost their opportunity to obtain eternal life.
*God cannot be mocked or bribed.   Men must repent or be
damned.*   It means, therefore, more to be a Christian
than simply to be sorry, or to be baptized, or to join
the church.   There are many who have done these
things who never forsook sin.   John the Baptist commanded the churchmen of his day to " Bring forth
therefore fruits meet for repentance."   What many
call repentance is like a walk through a barren or-
chard; there is a great rustle of the leaves, but on
looking up there is no fruit to be seen.

Mark begins his Gospel thus : " The beginning of the
gospel of Jesus Christ, the Son of God."   He then goes
on to tell us what that beginning is, " John did baptize in the wilderness, and preach the baptism of repentance for the remission of sins."   Repentance is
the beginning, and without it water-baptism amounts
to nothing.   Without an absolute abandonment of sin,
baptism is blasphemy.   The devil is just as fit a subject for baptism as the man who does not forsake sin.
Some sects baptize any one who will say, " I believe
Jesus is the Christ."   If this is the prerequisite to baptism, then the devils were fit subjects, for they confessed Christ.

Is this the doctrine now being preached in the

churches? We see many urged to sign cards, hold up
the hand, join the church, etc. But do we often hear
a seeking sinner faithfully instructed to renounce all
his sins, to bring forth fruits meet for repentance, to
restore what he has taken by fraud, to set right the
slander his tongue has been engaged in? Zaccheus
restored fourfold. "If the wicked restore the pledge,
give again that he had robbed, walk in the statutes of
life, without committing iniquity; he shall surely live,
he shall not die" (*Ezek. xxxiii.* 15). This always has
been, is, and always will be, the condition of becoming
a Christian. God is not mocked; and anything less
than this, be it ever so popular, produces only a bastard
Christianity, which will make its bed in hell.

II. *Faith.*

St. James tells us that the nature of saving faith was
misunderstood in the time of the apostles. It is quite
possible, then, that it may not be understood by every
one now, living nineteen centuries after the apostles.
Saving faith, like repentance, has its counterfeits, because it is the work of the devil to prevent the Christian life if possible.

1. *Saving faith is more than intellectual assent to
truth.* — Men may be perfectly orthodox in their creed,
and yet fail to become Christians, because saving faith
is an exercise of the heart rather than of the head. To
be sure, an intellectual faith is implied in saving faith,
for no one will exercise a faith of heart in that which
he believes does not exist. But one may have simply
an intellectual faith, and remain a devil. The devils
are more orthodox in their beliefs than many preachers.
There is a class of people who pronounce fit for bap-

tism those who confess with their mouths that they
believe Jesus is the Christ.   This would also make
the devils fit subjects for baptism ; for they confessed,
" Thou art the Christ."   But Jesus did not invite or
command them to be baptized.   " Thou believest there
is one God ; thou doest well : the devils also believe, and
tremble."   It is possible to have the head all right and
the heart all wrong.

2. *Saving faith is the reception of Jesus Christ by the
affections and will.* — This is what Paul means when he
says, " With the heart man believeth unto righteousness."   The Bible gives two definitions of faith.   It
defines it to be "the substance of things hoped for."
That is, the confident anticipation of things hoped for.
This is passive faith.   It also defines it actively thus,
" As many as received him, to them gave he power to
become the sons of God, even to them that believe on
his name."   Faith actively receives Jesus Christ to be
our "prophet, priest, and king ; " receives him in the
sense of taking all the responsibility that comes from
receiving him ; receives him as the only way of salvation ; receives him as the only way, and thus forsakes
every other way of salvation ; receives him as the only
hope, which, if it go down, we go down with it.   Faith
is the risking of our all for time and eternity on him.
It cries, —

> " Hangs my helpless soul on thee."

It will be seen at once how different this is from mere
mental assent to the truth that Jesus Christ is divine.
This kind of faith men are exercising every day.   This
is the basis of the healing art.   A sick man may be-

lieve in the skill of the physician to heal him; but this is merely mental, and does not cure him. But he may go a step farther, and put himself in the hands of the physician, and obey his orders; and in so doing he exercises saving faith. Otherwise the doctor cannot cure him. Just so we exercise saving faith by yielding ourselves wholly to Jesus, and receiving him to save us; and he gives us the "right and privilege to become the sons of God."

CHAPTER III.

EXPRESSION.

"Went about doing good." — ACTS x. 38.

IT was said of the first Christian that he "went about doing good." All his followers do the same. Not to endeavor to do good is not to be a Christian. The doing good here spoken of is not to be confined merely to charitable deeds. It includes the performance of good acts. But this is only one side of the question. He employed his whole time in doing good. Consequently he did no evil. All that he did was good. He committed no sin, either of omission or commission, whether in thought, word, or action.

There is much dispute to-day as to whether his followers can maintain the life that he maintained. Some declare it is impossible, — that we cannot refrain from sinning. If this be true, then certainly it is no use to attempt it. No one strives very earnestly for the impossible.

But we have seen that a Christian is a partaker of the divine nature. He has spiritual life in his soul. If that spiritual life will not enable him to do all that he ought to do, and leave undone all that he ought not to do, then the worldling has just as good an expectation of overcoming sin as he. If the divine nature does not enable the child of God to keep all his Father's commands, if he cannot refrain from doing some of the works of the devil, then the new life within is not divine life. The Word of God declares that the children of God do the works of their Father, and the children of the devil do the works of their father. If the children of God are not sufficiently empowered to keep from committing sin, then the power of the devil is stronger than the divine life in the child of God. This is the logical conclusion of the cry of modern Christianity, that "We cannot live without committing sin."

It may be well to accurately define sin right here. Mistakes are not sins. We are not culpable for mistakes. God does not hold us guilty for our mistakes. If mistakes were sins, then we should not be Christians at all if we made mistakes; for "whosoever committeth sin is of the devil." "Whoever is born of God doth not commit sin." The New Testament does not consider him a guilty sinner who only makes mistakes or errors of judgment. Lyman Abbott says of the Greek word *Harmatano*, which is the most frequently translated *to commit sin*, in the New Testament, "It signifies in the New Testament *moral wrong*, never a mere error in judgment." This definition may be relied upon among scholars.

The motive constitutes the quality of the action. "As a man thinketh in his heart, so is he." Hence two men may commit precisely the same act, and in one it will be a virtue, in the other a sin. For example, two men give the same amount of money to help the poor; one man does it to gain the reputation of being liberal in order to help his business, or because he is running for office. The other man gives the same amount for the same object — the poor ; but he does it from a good motive — pity for those in need.   We call the act of the first man hypocrisy, one of the most contemptible acts of which man is capable.   The other man's act we regard as a virtue, and yet the external act is the same.   It all depends upon the motive.   A Christian does duty from the right motive by the help of the divine life in him.   And he loves God too much to disobey him.   When we say he does not commit sin, therefore, we mean he does not wilfully break the commands of God.   He walks up to the light God gives him, and is anxious for more light.   The Psalmist in *Psalm xix.* makes these distinctions thus, " Who can understand his errors ? cleanse thou me from secret faults.   Keep back thy servant also from presumptuous sins ; let them not have dominion over me : then shall I be upright, and I shall be innocent from the great transgression."   Here we note the distinction between errors and presumptuous sins.   If we do not commit the latter, we shall not be guilty of " the great transgression," or the unpardonable sin.   We believe it to be in harmony with a reasonable interpretation of the Scriptures to assert that real Christians live without committing sin, for several reasons.

I. *God certainly requires as much after conversion as he did to prepare for conversion.* — He requires that in order to be converted, we stop our sinning.   This is the first step.   This is repentance, as we have already shown.   No person ever did get converted who did not abandon sin.   This is the inexorable law of God, which he will change for no one.   He has no favorites.   Men may join the church, and rise high in its offices ; but unless they forsook sin they never have been converted. And God certainly requires as much after conversion. "As ye have received the Lord Jesus Christ, so walk ye in him." If abandonment of sin is necessary to become converted, the abandonment must continue in order to remain converted. *One* sin cost Adam his home in Paradise, and brought trouble to the world; and can God retain in his favor to-day those who sin? Has he changed his principles of government or hatred of sin? "Whosoever shall keep the whole law and yet offend in one point, he is guilty of all." This matter of being a Christian is more serious than is commonly supposed.

2. *No one was ever compelled to commit sin.* — No one will ever be able to plead at the bar of God, "I could not do otherwise than sin." If we cannot keep from sin, then we have no freedom of will, but must sin because we were created to sin. If we were created to sin, then our Creator is responsible for so creating us. This makes God the author of sin, which is blasphemy. With the freedom of the will stands or falls the justice of God. He who says he cannot refrain from sin throws the responsibility upon God, and makes him the biggest sinner in the universe. God cannot punish us justly for what we cannot avoid. But the Word of God teaches an entirely different doctrine. "God is faithful, who will not suffer you to be tempted above that ye are able; but will with the temptation also make a way to escape, that ye may be able to bear it." This being true, no man can truthfully say, "I cannot help committing sin."

3. *That religion is vain that does not enable man to do*

as he ought. — If it does not enable him to do what he
ought to do, and leave undone what he ought not to
do, it is a weak affair, and unworthy of Almighty God.
Unless it makes a difference in the life, it is not worth
having.   He who has a religion that does not now enable him to do right, would never miss that religion
if he lost it.   The reason the world pick at flaws in
the church, and endeavor to find out and expose incon-
sistent professors of religion, is because they would like
to prove that there is no divine power to enable a man
to live as he ought.   If God will not enable us thus to
live, then the infidel has the best of the argument ; for
he knows the Bible teaches a righteous life, and he has
a right to demand the samples.

It has come to pass in many places that about all the
idea men have of the atonement is that it means salvation from hell.   The chief passages of Scripture that
speak of the atonement hardly refer to it as an escape
from punishment.   It is a larger salvation than that.
It is deliverance from sin, which is the cause of hell.
" Thou shalt call his name Jesus ; because he shall save
his people from their sins."   This is a grander salvation than escape from hell.   " Who gave himself for
us, that he might redeem us from all iniquity, and purify
unto himself a peculiar people, zealous of good works."
" The Lamb of God, which taketh away the sin of the
world."   "Jesus, that he might sanctify the people with
his own blood, suffered without the gate."   By saving
his people from sin, he saves from sin's punishment.
The man who keeps the statutes of the State never
stops to argue as to the existence of the penitentiary.
Practically there is no penitentiary for him.   God pro-

poses through the death of Jesus to save us from sin. And being saved from sin, we shall also be saved from its result, — hell.

The religion that does not save us from sinning, certainly is not very promising as to salvation from hell. We should not wish to take the risk for the future unless we had a present salvation. If Jesus Christ does not now save from sin, how do we know that he will save from hell by and by ?

4. *The Scripture teaches that this is the distinguishing characteristic of the children of God.* — This is the point in which they differ from the children of the wicked one — in not sinning.

Sin is "the works of the devil." It is thus rightly named because he first practised sin, and has been practising it ever since he first sinned. Sin is of the devil, because all who practise sin have his help. The children of the devil practise his works. On the other hand, holiness and righteousness have God as their origin and helper. The children of God do the works of God, and the children of the devil do the works of the devil. How absurd to assert that the children of God must practise the works of the devil !

There must, therefore, be this clear, definite, and eternal difference and distinction between Christians and the unregenerate world.

This view is so in harmony with common sense that it has passed into a proverb that "Prayer will make us leave off sinning, or sin will make us leave off praying." And yet multitudes of professed Christians believe they *must* sin.

5. *A religion that will not keep us from committing*

sin is below heathen philosophy. — The best heathen, under the light of nature, without the light of the atoning sacrifice and teachings of Jesus Christ, did as well as that. By their self-denial and abstinence they lived better than some so-called Christians believe possible. Adam Clarke, in his notes on 1 *John iii.* 9, says, " We have the most indubitable evidence that many of the heathen philosophers had acquired, by mental discipline and cultivation, an entire ascendency over all their wonted vicious habits. Perhaps my reader will remember the story of the physiognomist, who, in coming into the place where Socrates was lecturing, his pupils, wishing to put the principles of the man's science to proof, desired him to examine the face of their master and say what his moral character was. After a full contemplation of the philosopher's visage, he pronounced him 'the most gluttonous, drunken, brutal, and libidinous old man that he had ever met.' As the character of Socrates was the reverse of all this, his disciples began to insult the physiognomist. Socrates interfered and said, ' The principles of his science may be very correct, *for such I was, but I have conquered it by my philosophy.'* O ye Christian divines, ye real or pretended gospel ministers, will ye allow the influence of the grace of Christ a sway not even so extensive as that of the philosophy of a heathen who never heard of the true God ? "

6. *To deny this makes it easier to sin.* — If it be taught that we cannot live thus, it cuts the nerve of all effort to the contrary. Where is the man that is inspired to keep from sinning if he believes he cannot ? Only madmen attempt that which is impossible. What is the use to make effort against sin, if we know we cannot avoid

it? There is no need for any pulpit (as some do) to tell people they cannot live without committing sin. The devil is preaching that doctrine all the time, and he has done it so effectually that he does not need the help of religious teachers in this particular. If we are not as soldiers of Christ enlisted for victory, then what are we enlisted for? Some have supposed it means only final victory. But it is a present victory. He who does not have present, constant victory in the world, where the enemy is, need expect no final victory.

7. *A Christian keeps the commandments of Jesus Christ because he loves to do them.* — Jesus himself ·made this the test of true religion. "If ye love me, keep my commandments." "If a man love me, he will keep my words." This, coming from so high an authority, — the founder of Christianity himself, — shows that we can keep his commandments. We know there are those who think this impossible, but argue for sin, which is the breaking of the commandments of Jesus; yet his dictum is authority here.

There are those who think that it is a difficult matter to live thus. They talk about it being a hard thing to live a Christian life. They say they break the commandments of God "in thought, word, and deed" every day. This is a singular sentiment, strangely in contrast to the teachings of Jesus. He says, "My yoke is easy and my burden is light." If this be so, it is not difficult to keep his commandments. Love for Jesus constrains true Christians to keep his commandments. And if they keep his commandments, they are not breaking them. John says, "This is the love of God, that we keep his commandments: and his commandments are not grievous." It is a libel on Christianity, then, to say it is hard to keep the commandments, or, in other words, that we cannot refrain from committing sin. The love of God in every one who has spiritual life enables such an one to live in obedience, and with a real love for the will of God, so that he prefers it to his own will, and always prefers and yields to the will of God from choice. Real Christianity is divine life in the soul, and that divine life enables us to obey God because we love him.

A Christian has the supernatural within him; and the supernatural leads him to obey God in all things, not from compulsion, but from choice.

This expression of spiritual life enables the Christian to fulfil the apostolic injunction, "that ye may be blameless and harmless, the sons of God without rebuke, in the midst of a crooked and perverse nation, among whom ye shine as lights in the world." David says of such, "They also do no iniquity."

CHAPTER IV.

AFFECTIONS AND DESIRES.

"The love of God is shed abroad in our hearts by the Holy Ghost."
ROM. v. 5.

IT is said by the Apostle Paul, that "if any man be in Christ, he is a new creature." By this figure of speech we are to understand that there is something newly created. This new creation is not of the body or mind, but has sprung up in the spiritual nature of man. There is a something not found there previously. By this new creation is meant the creation of new desires and affections, such as were never before possessed. He now "loves what he once hated, and hates that which he once loved." There has come about a revolution and transformation in his spiritual and moral nature.

He has received "a new heart." That is, he has a love he never had before. "The love of God is shed abroad in his heart by the Holy Ghost."

To change a man's natural tastes is remarkable. For instance, a man cannot endure even the thought of eating a certain kind of food because it is distasteful to him. Suppose all of a sudden he gets an intense liking for it; this is marvellous. But when a man who has no love for God has injected into his soul a love for God and rightness such as he has never felt or dreamed of as possible, it is a still greater marvel.

I. *This love is supernatural.*

It is the love of God. It is the same love that dwells
in the bosom of the Almighty. It would be impossible
to be a partaker of the divine nature without being a
partaker of the divine love, for " God is love." In the
Greek the term for divine love (*Agape*) is always different from another term (*Phila*) used to denote all other
kinds of love. It is not the same as conjugal, parental,
or filial love. It is a term that always denotes a different kind of love. No man is born with this love until
he is born the second time. Then God lets fall into
the heart of man a drop of that infinite ocean of love,
and this is the new heart. This may develop, and swell
into an ocean of its own. In a thousand ways it is different from human, natural love. It is as different from
the love that the natural man possesses as light from
darkness. The natural man loves his kind, his family
and friends, as the animal does his kind, from natural
causes. But supernatural love is something beyond
and beside all this. Let us notice the contrast between
natural and spiritual love.

1. *A Christian loves God.* — He does not try to love
God, but he loves him. The natural man admires the
works of God, but he often mistakes love for admiration. Men prate about the Fatherhood of God, and
about "seeing God in nature," who have no more respect for him than the admiration that we feel for a
great artist or architect as we view his works. We
may admire the works of a man whose character we
cannot love. But a Christian, being a partaker of the
divine nature, loves that being who has imparted that
nature to him as naturally as he once loved sin. Unsaved men admire and fear (in a slavish sense) God,

but do not love him. This is true, because the test of love is obedience; and unsaved men are not obedient. Their so-called love breaks down right here. They do not love him, for if they did they would forsake sin for his sake. If they loved God, they would love the things he loves, and hate the things he hates.

2. *A Christian loves everything that is good.* — Here we notice the contrast between the two classes. The natural man sees little that is attractive in the Word of God. To be sure, he sometimes admires its literary beauties; but there are few even of that class. Otherwise, he cares little for this book. But a Christian loves the Bible. It stirs his heart to its depths as he reads it. What good food is to the palate the Word of God is to his soul. He feels that it "is sweeter than honey." The natural man never prays unless he is in trouble; but the Christian prays, not only because he desires certain requests, but also because he delights to pray. He holds communion with God as with a dear friend. An unsaved man takes little delight in the house of God. He goes there from habit, duty, or for profit. But the Christian feels that a day in the courts of God is "better than a thousand." This contrast is because of the different natures of the two men. It is a matter of taste or disposition.

3. *Vice versa, a Christian has no relish for worldly frivolities.* — When he became converted, the language of Charles Wesley was the language of his heart : —

"Vain, delusive world, adieu,
  With all of creature good !
  Only Jesus I pursue,
  Who bought me with his blood.

All thy pleasures I forego ;
I trample on thy wealth and pride ;
Only Jesus will I know,
And Jesus crucified."

A Christian does not have to resist the inclination to go to the world for pleasure. He finds his comfort and happiness in the love of God shed abroad in his heart. He does not have to go abroad for a feast ; he finds it at home. The professed Christian who says, " There is no harm in the theatre," " I see no harm in dancing," who argues for these things, has made a mistake in supposing himself a Christian. Had he become a partaker of the divine nature, these things would be tasteless and useless. We can tell whether we are real Christians or not by what we like, for that reveals our nature. There are people who say it does not hurt their religion to dance or attend the theatre. We agree with them. Any kind of religion that seeks its satisfaction from the same things that the unsaved world gets its happiness from, cannot be true religion. It never hurts paper flowers to be put out in a frosty night. It never injures a buzzard to feed on carrion. There is no perfume in paper flowers, and the flesh of the buzzard is itself tainted. Let us examine ourselves in the light of this proposition : to which does our love go, the things of God, or the frivolities of this world ? " No man can serve two masters." " Ye cannot serve God and mammon." Jesus did not say we ought not, but we *cannot*, serve God and mammon. It is a moral impossibility. We serve that which we love. Our love reveals what we are. All this follows naturally from the definition of a Christian. The divine nature within causes him to love those things that harmonize with the divine nature, and hate those things that are hostile to the nature of God. For a good lover also means a good hater.

4. *A Christian has a peculiar love for the people of God.* — "We know that we have passed from death unto life because we love the brethren." There is a peculiar love for God's people. It is closer and more intimate than even the ties of flesh and blood. Our kindred many times cannot understand our experience. Sometimes relatives have turned against their friends who have become Christians. But there is such a bond between true Christians that they have a fellowship unknown to mere flesh and blood. Jesus said, "Whosoever shall do the will of my Father which is in heaven, the same is my brother and sister and mother." Here are ties stronger and more sacred than those that bind families together. These are the bonds of "the household of faith." Many a soul, misunderstood by companions in the flesh, finds that he is understood by those who have obtained like precious faith.

5. *A Christian loves his neighbor as himself.* — This does not mean that he loves his neighbor as he does the members of the household of faith, or as he loves his most intimate friends. He is not required so to do. But he loves himself aright, and loves his neighbor the same way — in a right manner. Paul explains this by saying, "Love worketh no ill to his neighbor." Just as when a man loves himself properly he will do nothing intentionally to injure himself, so, too, he will do nothing to injure his neighbor. He will seek to "please his neighbor, for his good to edification." The last

word means to build up. On the one hand, he will not injure his neighbor; on the other, he will seek to build him up in righteousness. This is the love that a Christian has for his neighbor. And Jesus told us that our neighbor is the person who is in need of our help.

6. *A Christian loves his enemies.* — This is the crowning glory of Christianity. It marks the difference between a true Christian and all other classes of people in the world. The man who says "I cannot love my enemies," has not yet had the love of God dropped into his bosom from heaven. He professed the religion of Jesus, but has not yet become a Christian. He thought he was a Christian because he kneeled at the altar, was baptized, and joined the church. He considered himself a Christian because the preacher, perhaps, said so. But he never yet became a partaker of the divine nature. Because, if he had received that, it would be natural for him to act like his Master, who said, "If ye love them which love you, what reward have ye? do not even the publicans the same?" Any one can love those that love him. But it requires the nature of him who died praying for his enemies to love as he did. Natural love loves those that love it. Supernatural love loves those who are enemies. By this we may know whether we are real Christians or not. People sometimes think they are Christians, who are deceived in so thinking. We have yet to hear of one who ever was deceived in the matter if he applied this test. Hear what the first Christian said, " Love your enemies, bless them that curse you, do good to them which hate you, and pray for them which despitefully use you, and persecute you; that ye may be the children of your Father

which is in heaven." If church-membership were sifted out by this rule, where would modern Christendom find itself! And yet this is pure Christianity according to Christ. "If any man have not the spirit of Christ, he is none of his." He who cannot love his enemies has yet to obtain the new heart. Is it not a great experience to be a child of God! to be regenerated and justified in his sight! Entire sanctification is a great experience. But no one need think that in order to find a place for it, we must consider regeneration as a small or unelevated experience. It is a high and holy experience to be born of God. It enables us to love our enemies, and to do good to all men. Depend upon it, real Bible regeneration is a scarce article. Were there more of it, there would be more seekers of entire sanctification. Many people contend against the latter simply because they never had the former. Regeneration according to the teaching of Jesus Christ is almost as rare as entire sanctification. Let us be sure we have regeneration before we seek entire sanctification.

II. *A real Christian has a most intense desire for a pure heart.*

Anything that is pure contains nothing else contrary to its nature. A pure heart is the new heart with nothing contrary to that new heart. It is the love of God in the soul with nothing contrary to love. All evil tempers, dispositions, and qualities are absent from a pure heart. A Christian loves holiness because he has the divine nature. And for the same reason he hates sin. And he hates sin in himself the most, because he has the opportunity of knowing its workings the better in himself than anywhere else. He can never rest satis-

fied while there is anything in his heart that is contrary
to that divine love that glows there.   God cannot look
upon sin with the least degree of allowance, and the
divine nature within us must instinctively recoil at sinful dispositions.   Indeed, sin is a weight hung upon the
neck of the soul where the love of God is shed abroad.
It hinders.   It disturbs.   It hurts at times.   Even when
it does not get the mastery over love, yet it is a hindrance to the development of love.   But when it causes
the Christian to break down, it is even more to be hated
and feared.   So every true Christian wants to get rid
of this Jonah, and can never feel really at peace until
he is cast out.   Jesus declared that the Christian has a
most intense desire for holiness.   He put it under the
figure of hunger and thirst.   "Blessed are they which
do hunger and thirst after righteousness."   This is not
the state of a sinner.   The latter does not hunger and
thirst after righteousness.   It requires the new birth
to put into the heart an intense desire for holiness.
Becoming a new creature puts into the soul a desire
for holiness.   Let us for a moment, then, see just what
is meant by righteousness.   *It means that state of heart
that is right.*   It does not mean about right.   We hear
people declaring that they are about right.   But that
is not right.   Nothing can be more or better than right.
And that which is less than that is wrong.   As some
one says, "It is the state of being upright, downright,
outright, inright, and all right."   It means freedom from
sin.   Paul says, "Awake to righteousness and sin not."
The divine command is, "Break off your sins by righteousness."   "Being made free from sin, ye became the
servants of righteousness."   We see from these pas-

sages, then, that it means the state of being free from sin. In other words, every Christian has an intense desire to be free from sin. This is another test, then, that we must apply to our experience to ascertain if we are real Christians. To be free from sin is to be right. Can any one conceive of a Christian praying or desiring to be anything less than this ? Can we suppose a real Christian praying, " O Lord, I want to be almost right, but not quite "?

Hunger and thirst are the most intense appetites which we possess. When they are not satisfied they turn men into brutes and fiends. There is nothing more awful than extreme thirst in all the possibilities of human suffering. These are daily and constantly recurring appetites. They are not merely occasional. So that when Jesus uses this figure he means an intense, constant, and habitual desire for holiness. Not something occasional ; not a wish, but an intensity of desire. There are some things that should not be mistaken for this intensity of purpose.

1. *The desire of the awakened sinner.* — This is not hungering and thirsting after righteousness. The sinner who has real conviction can think of nothing else but how to get rid of his load of guilt. He has no time to think of purity of heart. He is like the ancient runner to the city of refuge. Justice is on his track. How shall he escape justice ? He thinks only of getting into the city. He thinks but little of the beauties of the city, or the rights and privileges of citizenship, or how he shall live. His chief concern is to get in. So the convicted sinner has something else to think of besides the blessing of holiness. The man who thinks we are

wholly sanctified when converted shows that he does not know what conversion is. The sinner's chief concern is pardon. The Christian's is purity.

2. *Nor is it to have a great experience.* — A real Christian wants to be holy, not because it is a great and glorious experience, but because he is in love with holiness, and nothing else can satisfy his nature. A hungry man wants food, not because it is a good thing, nor because it is "the proper thing" to be well fed, but because it satisfies an intense desire of his nature, so intense that he feels he *must* have it. People who seek holiness in order to have a great experience, or to be happy, never get it. They need to be converted, for it is the regenerated man who has a real passion for holiness. Such a man desires holiness, whether people consider it a small or great experience.

3. *Nor is it a desire for an experience like that of some one else.* — A real hungry man wants food, not because other people have it, but because he needs it, and cannot get along without it. The glowing experiences of others may make him hopeful that God will satisfy *him*, but he does not seek it in order to be like them. He wants to be like Jesus. He does not want it to be like others, but because he feels he will perish without it. He who wants holiness of heart in order to be like some one else in experience, needs to be born again. Then he will obtain an insatiable desire for holiness for his soul's sake.

4. *Nor is it a desire for holiness because it is popular.* — Hungry men do not think about the popularity or unpopularity of the food, but how to get at it. They want the food anyway. A real thirsty man seeking

strong drink cares little for his reputation. He wants satisfaction, whether it be popular or not. A real Christian wants holiness for its own sake, whether it be popular or otherwise. His question is not, whether " the rulers have believed on him," but " Is there such an experience as having sin all removed from the heart ? If there is, tell me how to get it, and I will pay the price, because I hate sin, and long to be as near like my Master as I can." A true Christian wants to be holy, whether any one else does or not. This is the reason that people pray for holiness when they are in a clear experience of regeneration. We used to hear the brethren in our boyhood, when they were at the glowing point of their prayer, say, "Cleanse us from the last and least remains of sin." The reason people so pray is because they have the assistance of the Holy Spirit, —the Spirit of holiness, — who urges them on. He helps all true praying. "For we know not what we should pray for as we ought : but the Spirit itself maketh intercession for us with groanings which cannot be uttered." The Spirit of holiness could not be consistent with himself and inspire us to pray for less than that holiness which " is the will of God concerning us." Many years ago we learned a hymn which expresses the aim of every real Christian. We give one stanza : —

" How happy is the man
Who hath chosen Wisdom's ways,
And measured out his span
To his God in prayer and praise.
His God and his Bible
Are all that he desires;
To holiness of heart
He continually aspires."

How are multitudes deceiving themselves. They think they are Christians, but do not desire to be holy. They have not the nature of God, which constitutes a true Christian ; for if they had, they would intensely desire to be free from sin.

Rev. James Caughey, an evangelist through whom God shook three nations, says of this desire for purity of heart, " It is the highest gem that sparkles in *real* justification. Solomon says, ' A virtuous woman is a crown to her husband.' Purity is the crown of justification. If it be genuine, this desire is always attached to it, — as weight is to lead, as heat is to fire, as fragrance to the rose, as green to a healthy leaf, — inseparable."

From all these considerations we are logically brought to the conclusion that *a real Christian is a specialist upon the subject of holiness.* The charge has usually been made, that only one class of people are specialists on the question of holiness, — those who profess the second blessing. But if we understand the nature, affections, and desires of Christians, every one is a specialist in seeking, obtaining, and retaining a holy heart, and in urging others to the same. The man who is not a specialist on this subject has lost the freshness and keen edge of his first love, if he ever had it. There never yet was a real convert in his earliest love who was not desirous of holiness, — even if he did not know it by that name. How often people are scared away from holiness by being afraid of being known as " specialists."

A real hungry man is a specialist on the subject of food. And a real Christian is specially hungry for the specialty of the Bible — holiness. They who can be driven away from seeking holiness by being afraid of being known as specialists, had better take account of stock, and see where they are. A real Christian makes a specialty of getting to heaven. In order to do so, he will desire to make a specialty of holiness, which is the only thing that will keep him out of hell. A man who can be scared away from a feast by being called names is not yet very hungry. And a professed Christian who can be frightened, flattered, or cajoled from seeking holiness, needs to seek a clear evidence that he is a child of God. It is a great experience, again we repeat, to be a Christian, to keep justified before God.

CHAPTER V

A GOOD HOPE.

" We are saved by hope." — ROM. viii. 24.

WHEN Israel had crossed the Jordan, and laid siege to the city of Ai, they were defeated, much to their surprise. The sin of one man caused this disastrous defeat. Detected, accused, and overwhelmed with shame, Achan confessed his sin in transgressing the command of God, and thus bringing disaster to the whole church. Sentence of death was passed upon Achan because of his treason. Achan, with all his possessions, was taken to a valley and destroyed. Above him was raised a monument of stones. " Wherefore the name of that place was called, The valley of Achor." (*Josh. vii.* 26.) The meaning is, *The valley of trouble.* Nearly seven hundred years after this, God through his servant Isaiah makes the valley of Achor, with its trouble, a place for hope ; and many years after, through another prophet (*Hos. ii.* 15), he says he will give a backsliding people "the valley of Achor as a door of hope." He would make the valley of trouble, which had been cursed by being the place of punishment for crime, a door of hope, through which they might enter into future blessing. The valley of Achor had been a door of hope to Joshua and Israel, because, obeying God there, they could expect future victory. This world is a valley of Achor. Here is trouble because of disobedience and sin. But right here in the midst of trouble God makes "the valley of Achor a door of hope" to those who obey him. We hear much said about "a good hope," "a false hope," "indulging a hope," etc. It is quite important that we understand the nature of Christian hope.

It is remarkable that, while hope is a characteristic of Christian experience, yet it is not found in the catalogue of the fruits of the Spirit, as given by Paul in the Epistle to the Colossians. The reason for this seems to be that hope is rather the result of the working of faith, which is the fruit of the Spirit. "Faith is the substance (foundation, — that which stands under) of things hoped for." Faith is the foundation, and hope is the temple built upon the foundation of faith. He who has a real faith erects upon it the observatory of hope, from whose heights he views the glories of the world to come. His telescope views the skies, and revels in the glories of the life to come. Hope always has regard to the future. A genuine Christian hope is a great stimulus to patient endurance of present ills and trials. "If it were not for hope the heart would break." It is this that cheers the struggling saint, and gives him fresh courage to battle on "a few more days or years at most," expecting the glories of the future world.

> "This glorious hope revives
> Our courage by the way;
> While each in expectation lives,
> And longs to see the day."

The hope of a Christian is of gaining heaven with all its joys; of escaping hell with all its miseries. This brings present peace and happiness. But the Word of God speaks of certain kinds of hope that are false and deceptive. "The hypocrite's hope shall perish." "The hope of unjust men perisheth." Nearly all the prominent churchmen of the time of Jesus had hope; but it was built upon the sand, and failed them at the last. These churchmen were perfectly familiar with the Scriptures, and yet failed to gain eternal life. A good hope is likened by Paul to the anchor that holds the ship on the stormy sea. It was hope that led Moses to forsake the treasures of Egypt, Abraham to leave his father's house and native land. They looked for something better. How, then, shall we distinguish between a good and a false hope? We reply, that hope rests on two things : 1, Present experience ; 2, Adjustment to the hoped-for future. Experience worketh hope, according to Paul. The experience of present salvation is a pledge of future salvation. God gives us a present salvation, which enables us to believe that he will give us final salvation. The basis of a Christian hope is the merits of Jesus Christ, and present experience enables us to feel that his blood now avails for us. We said adjustment to the hoped-for future. The man who expects future good seeks to prepare for that future good. He is getting ready for it, living as if he believed it a reality. The ploughman breaks the soil and drops the seed, but he also prepares the granary into which he expects to gather the harvest. Those who have a good hope do not thereby become careless and presumptuous ; they still seek to make their "calling and election sure." But they are acting so that their hope may not be dimmed or become mere presumption. Instead of making them careless, it makes them more earnest than ever. Just as when a traveller sails for another country which he expects to reach, he secures his passport, exchanges his money for the kind used there, provides the kind of garments adapted to the climate, so he who has a good hope of heaven is looking carefully to see if he has the fitness for it, lest he be deceived after all. The old-time Calvinists only dared to "indulge a hope," they were so fearful of being deceived. God tells us whether we have a good hope or not. We may find his test in the Bible. If we are seeking with earnest hunger the fitness that he gives for heaven, then we have a good hope. How, then, do we know we have a hope that will stand the testing of the last day? 1, By the possession of a present salvation; 2, By a sincere determination to be fully prepared for eternal glory. We may have a good experience and rest in that, and fail in our hope; therefore God tells us plainly, "*Every man that hath this hope in him* [Jesus] *purifieth himself even as he is pure.*" Here is the test of a good hope in Jesus. We wish these words could sink into the heart of every professed Christian in this world. Let no man deceive himself. The man who has not a pure heart, and is not seeking it with all his soul, has no good hope of eternal salvation. Is not this Scripture plain? Let us measure ourselves by the Word of God. Here it is. God has called us to holiness. There will be multitudes deceived and lured on by false hopes, only to be undeceived in the last day. They looked upon holiness as fanaticism, as a twist in the brain of visionary people. With Bibles in their houses, they refused to believe "Without holiness no man shall see the Lord." They

scorned the call to holiness. They tried to make themselves believe that being once converted, and being baptized, and joining the church, was enough. They failed,
not because they were not once converted, but because
they stopped in their course, and refused to let God
purify their hearts. Reader, be sure you have a good
hope. Be sure it is according to the Word of God. He
cares more for what he has written in his Word than for
all the past experience he has given you. Take this
passage of Scripture, "Every man that hath this hope in
him purifieth himself even as he is pure." Make it the
straight-edge that you shall lay up beside your hope,
and see if it be in harmony with it. Depend upon it,
if you are a real Christian, you either have a heart from
sin set free, or you are intensely seeking it.

CHAPTER VI.

THE PATH OF LIGHT.

" The path of the just is as the shining light, that shineth more and more unto the perfect day." — PROV. iv. 18.

TRUE Christians belong to the kingdom of light. The apostle calls them " children of the light," because they are children of God, who " is light," and in them there is no darkness at all. The difference between them and the worldling is, they have been translated out of the kingdom of darkness, and now walk in a path that grows brighter all the way. Let us trace their pathway.

I. *The Christian was once in darkness.*

This is the condition of the unsaved world to-day. "Darkness covers the earth, and gross darkness the people." This is moral darkness. By darkness is meant ignorance of God and his truth. This dense darkness is lighted up only where there are Christians, who are "the light of the world." Except there were some such, there could be no conceivable reason why God should keep this world in existence another moment. Isaiah, speaking of this state of things in the kingdom of Judah, says, "Except the Lord of hosts had left unto us a very small remnant, we should have been as Sodom, and like unto Gomorrah." But for these few faithful ones, society would have been like those cities whose uncleanness had so polluted the earth that God had to cleanse the very soil with fire. Modern society would break up but for the few who are " the salt of the earth," keeping it pure. Man by nature is totally depraved. When people hear depravity spoken of they misconceive its meaning. We do not mean by it that there is no good in man. There are many excellent traits that have survived the fall, relics of his former glory. But we mean that he is so far gone from original righteousness that of himself he never would desire to come back to God. But for the moving of God upon his heart, he would never have a desire to serve him. All desires to flee from the wrath to come, all light showing our lost condition and what we ought to be, come from the enlightenment of the Holy Spirit.

This is the crucial point. No doubt angels look with breathless interest to see if the convicted man yields to the light of conviction that God gives him. If he yields, God saves him, and brings him from the dawn of conviction into the glorious sunrise of the regenerated life. This is what Paul means as he says, " God, who commanded the light to shine out of darkness, hath shined in our hearts, to reveal the knowledge of the glory of God in the face of Jesus Christ." Charles Wesley beautifully expresses it thus : —

> " Long my imprisoned spirit lay,
> Fast bound in sin and nature's night.
> Thine eye diffused a quickening ray.
> I woke. My dungeon flamed with light!
> My chains fell off! My heart was free.
> I rose, went forth, and followed thee."

By agreeing with the light of conviction, we come thus into the light of regeneration. And henceforth the Christian is in the light. He is no more in darkness. Those who are in darkness are not Christians. " If we say we have fellowship with him, and walk in darkness, we lie, and do not the truth." He has escaped the darkness of sin and doubt and ignorance of God. They who are in the dark do not belong to the kingdom of light; for " God is light, and in him is no darkness at all." We must here, however, make a distinction between darkness and heaviness. Peter tells us that there is such a thing as " heaviness through manifold temptations." But this may exist without darkness. The Christian, as he looks towards God and heaven and the future, sees nothing but light. Like the Israelites in Goshen, he is in light, while the world about him are like the Egyptians, in darkness.

The Christian is not only in a pathway of light, but also of *increasing light*. As sure as we agree with the light God gives in awakening and conviction, he will lead us into the light of regeneration. And as sure as we come into the light of regeneration, he will give us greater light still. Light is the preface to more light, if we are true to God. For " the pathway of the just is as the shining light, that shineth more and more unto the perfect day."

There are people who say, " The Lord did it all for me when I was converted." No doubt he did all for them that he ever did at that time in the line of conversion ; but the man who makes that assertion makes a sad mistake, for true religion grows better, the path becomes brighter, and Jesus Christ improves upon acquaintance. The inspired author of the Epistle to the Hebrews says, " Leaving the principles of the doctrine of Christ, let us go on unto perfection." But how can the man who "got it all at conversion" go on to anything more? The Revised Version translates the passage thus, "Wherefore let us cease to speak of the first principles of Christ, and press on unto perfection." Wesley's comment upon the passage is, "Saying no more of them for the present." But this would spoil the religious stock in trade of many. All they can talk of is the time of their conversion. It seems to be the only bright spot in their lives. Their testimony is a reminiscence. A Christian finds it constantly better as he goes on. If it is not better than when he first believed, then he has stopped on the road; for it is more light or decreasing light. He is like a bicycle rider; when he stops, he *must* get off. No matter how glorious a conversion we have, it is the smallest end of the increasingly shining pathway in which the Christian travels. Were it anything less than increase, our spiritual powers would stagnate.

Increasing light has been the divine method throughout all the ages. This seems to be the reason that God schooled the world for four thousand years by the different dispensations, until, by the dispensations of the patriarchs, the law, the prophets, and of Jesus Christ, he finished with the dispensation of the Holy Ghost, in which we now live. In just the same way he has dispensations or epochs in the experience of the Christian. He is not like human theologians, who have to bolster up a theory. He leads his people on from grace to grace and from glory to glory. "We all, with open face beholding as in a glass the glory of the Lord, are changed into the same image from glory *to* glory, even as by the Spirit of the Lord."

There is a fulness of blessing that we come to in this increasing pathway of light, if we maintain our regenerated life. We call especial attention to a passage in *John i.* 16, "And of his fulness have all we received, and grace for grace." The term translated *fulness* here is the Greek *pleroma*. This word means literally *that which is put in to fill up whatever is lacking.* It is thus translated in *Matt. ix.* 16, "No man putteth a piece of new cloth unto an old garment, for *that which is put in to fill it up* taketh from the garment." Here *pleroma* is translated, *that which is put in to fill it up.* In the parallel passage in *Mark ii.* 21 it is translated, "The new piece that filleth it up." The fulness is, then, that blessing which fills up that which is lacking in our Christian life. That blessing that comes to supplement and complete the experience of regeneration is what Paul means when he speaks of "the fulness of the blessing of the gospel of Christ," a special experience filling all that we lack in our Christian experience. The remainder of the verse is also as explicit. It tells us the divine method of receiving the fulness thus, "grace *for* grace." This is a remarkable expression. By turning to the original, we find that the preposition *for* is *anti*, which means, *instead of.* For instance, the Pope of Rome is anti-Christ. He claims to rule *instead of*, or in the place of, Christ. We hear Jesus called the anti-type of all the types and shadows of the Old Testament economy. That is, he took their place. They ceased when he came. He existed in their stead, as they were no longer needed. We will give our readers one or two further instances in which this preposition in the Greek is used in the sense of *instead of.* "An

eye *for* an eye, and a tooth *for* a tooth " (*Matt. v.* 38).
This was the method of punishment under the old dispensation.   He who had put out the eye or tooth of another must himself offer the same member in place of
the one injured.   We give one other passage.   " The
Son of man came not to be ministered unto, but to minister, and to give his life a ransom *for* many," — a ransom in the stead of many.   We have shown, then, that
the preposition in the phrase " grace *for* grace " means
" grace taking the place of grace."   One state of grace
taking the place of another.   *The fulness* is obtained
when the grace of regeneration is superseded or com-
pleted by the grace of entire sanctification.   Whedon
comments on this passage thus, " Grace additionally
bestowed for grace improved."   Wesley says, " One
blessing upon another."   This is the normal method of
the real Christian life that God intends all converts to
be speedily led to.   He who has been true to the light
of regeneration will soon be led to feel the need of
something more ; and God will lead him into the fulness, if he is true and steadfast to his light, whether he
knows the name of it or not.   This is why all genuinely
converted souls have a relish for all the light God has
for them, and an appetite for holiness, even when they
have never heard of it by name.   And many a soul has
come into this glorious experience of heart purity, who
has come on the line of his needs, with no human
teacher.   We believe every genuine convert faces the
question of heart purity sooner or later by the unerring
teaching and leading of the Holy Spirit.   He must now
go on, and walk up to the greater light, or go back into
a life of sinning and repenting, as thousands have who

failed to follow the Spirit's leading. We are not talking
of an idealism, not at all! God intends that the fulness
shall be the normal experience of the Christian, and not
the "up and down" life we see and hear so much of.

We object to the term "Higher Life." It is simply
one way of dodging the Scriptural terms, *sanctification*
and *holiness*. The term "higher life" implies that there
are two kinds of Christian life, one high and the other
low, which we cannot accept. There is but one life, and
it is a high one of increasing light; it is agreement
with the light, and walking in it all the way. When
God shows us any new light, we walk up to it with glad-
ness, because we are in love with the light. When God
shows a truly regenerated soul the light of entire sanctification, he walks up to it gladly, and seeks it with
all his heart. He does not seek excuse for not coming
up to it. It is the people who are not regenerated that
fight holiness. *Every Christian walks in greater light
each day, and is seeking all the further light he can get.*
No preacher can preach too searching truth for him.
He loves the light. He says, "Turn on the light! I
want to be just as good as possible. I want to know
the worst of my case this side the judgment. I cannot afford to be mistaken. So turn on all the light you
can, dear Lord, and I will walk in it." No wonder, then,
that some such earnest souls have come into the fulness,
and had their hearts cleansed from all sin, who never
heard technically of the doctrine of holiness. They
prove the Scripture, "If we walk in the light as he is in
the light, we have fellowship one with another, and the
blood of Jesus Christ his Son cleanseth us from all sin."
A real Christian so loves the light that he will not let

anything, whether it be a friend, an associate, an indul-
gence, a habit, an amusement, or a prejudice, come between him and the light. He estimates the right and
wrong of everything by the effect it has on his *own* experience. He does not take the word of others for it,
but judges everything by its influence in increasing or
decreasing his light. It is said that Alexander the Great
went to see Diogenes the philosopher, and wishing to
patronize him, asked what he could do for him. " Just
please stand from between me and the sun," was the
reply. All he wanted of the king was to stand out of his
light. This is the attitude of the real Christian ; he
says to everybody and everything, " You must stand out
of my light," and everything and everybody that in any
way dims the light, he renounces.

This is where many lose their experience who once
rejoiced in the light. As surely as we do not receive
gladly and walk in the new light we have, we shall lose
that light. " Unto him that hath shall be given, and he
shall have abundance : but from him that hath not shall
be taken away even that which he hath." This was
the difficulty with the young man who came to Jesus.
He was a member of God's church. He had kept the
commandments. He had been walking up to his light.
Still, he felt dissatisfied. He longed for a degree of salvation that would satisfy him. He asked Jesus, " What
good thing must I do, that I may inherit eternal life?"
Jesus replied, " If thou wilt be perfect, sell that thou
hast, and follow me." Jesus saw that, in order to have
.perfect salvation, he must have the coveteousness of his
nature destroyed. He told him how to obtain it, — by a
complete consecration. This greater light he refused

to walk in. The result of it was, he went away from
Jesus. Thousands go away from Jesus right at this
point, by not going on into the greater light. This
was the difficulty with the Israelites. They had been
delivered from Egyptian oppression. They had special
revelation of the will of God. They had the tabernacle
of God among them. No people were ever so privi-
leged. Yet God had delivered them, not merely for the
purpose of getting them out of bondage, but of getting
them into all the glories of Canaan. Similarly, to-day,
God converts not merely to get us out of the world
and hell, but to get us into the glorious experience of
full salvation. "He led them out that he might lead
them in." So he led his people to the borders of Canaan; and they refused to go in, and forfeited their
birthright, which was prosperity in this present world.
They never had any. It is very significant what name
was given the place where they refused to go in. It
was *Kadesh*. We wonder that many people are blind
to-day, and do not see the significance of this word. It
means in the Hebrew *holiness*. God set up this word
kadesh, holiness, as a warning to the latter-day church,
and also a lesson. The Holy Ghost warns us to-day
of the *kadesh* to which he will lead his church, where it
must go on or go back. There is no other alternative.
If he had named the place where Israel stopped by
some other name there might be less excuse, but *holiness* is still the great stopping-place of thousands. We
may well ask why God gave the place this name, if it
does not mean something to us. It shows that he
meant to teach us that Canaan represented holiness,
and the journey of the Israelites to it meant the life of

the Christian before he gets to *holiness, kadesh* — the rest of the soul. The author of the Epistle to the Hebrews declares that their example is a warning to us, lest we fail to enter, not into heaven, but into "the rest which remaineth to the people of God." This is rest in this world, because he adds, "We which have believed *do* enter into rest." This is a present tense rest. Present disobedience will spoil past gain and advancement in the journey. It will take all the grace we can get to keep what we have. For example, a father sends his son to a school to prepare for college. The son makes a good record, and graduates with honor. The father is pleased. He says, "Well done, my boy. I am delighted with you. Now go to college." But the son objects and refuses. He says he has got enough education. Now, the father is grieved and displeased, not because the boy has not done well so far, but because he does not go on to the objective point which the father designed when he sent him to the preparatory school. Holiness, according to the Bible, is the experience to which we are called. God leads us into the experience of regeneration that we may have our eyes opened to see, and be prepared for entire sanctification ; but many say, "I have enough," or refuse to go on, and thus lose the favor of God, not because they have not been converted, but because they do not agree with their advanced light. For as surely as a Christian is a Christian by agreeing with the *initial* light God gave him, so sure he cannot remain a Christian except he agree with the *increasing* light God gives him. The time comes in the history of the Christian when he must become entirely sanctified in order to remain justified.

CHAPTER VII.

TITLE AND FITNESS.

"Which hath made us meet to be partakers of the inheritance of the saints in light." — COL. i. 12.

BEING a Christian constitutes heirship. Being a member of the family, we are heirs to our portion of the estate. This is not only true in common law, but also in the family of God. "If children," says Paul, "then heirs; heirs of God, and joint-heirs with Christ." The little Scotch maiden who was on her way to the secret place of meeting, and was stopped by the soldiery, who were endeavoring to break up such assemblies of worship, was asked where she was going. She replied, that her elder brother had died, and she was on her way to hear the will read and claim her portion. The soldiers allowed her to pass, wishing that she might get a generous portion. This answer of the maiden has been regarded by many as a very ingenious reply. But it was only the truth. What looks to be a very ingenious excuse to worldly minded people is a sober reality. It is no figure of rhetoric, or play of the imagination. We are heirs, so Peter declares, "to an inheritance incorruptible, undefiled, and that fadeth not away." In other words, an everlastingly pure inheritance in heaven. Charles Wesley says every Christian rejoices in the title to his future inheritance : —

> "How happy every child of grace
>   Who knows his sins forgiven.
>   This earth, he cries, is not my place;
>   I seek my place in heaven, —
>   A country far from mortal sight;
>   Yet, O! by faith I see
>   The land of rest, the saint's delight,
>   The heaven prepared for me."

He obtained the title to this inheritance, not by his good works, but because he is a member of the family. Here is where many make their mistake. They expect to earn heaven by their good works ; but it is ours, not because we deserve it, but because we have the divine nature ; we are the children of God. And estates are given to heirs, not for their works, not because they have earned them, but because they are of the family. The prince succeeds his father upon the throne, not for his wealth, not for his efforts at earning the throne, but because he has the royal blood in his veins. God makes us " kings and priests." The overcomers are to sit with Jesus upon the throne because they are partakers of the divine nature. Unless we are partakers of the divine nature we cannot be heirs. Here is where Universalism makes its mistake. It insists that all are the children of God. But the Word of God declares that some are the children of the devil. Paul says, by nature we " are the children of wrath." Hence we must be born again, and inherit the divine nature in order to be " heirs of God and joint-heirs with Jesus Christ."

Every Christian has his title-deed given him, telling him that he is a child of God in the witness of the Spirit. " Because ye are sons, God hath sent forth the Spirit of his Son into your hearts, crying, Abba, Father." This entrance of the Spirit into the heart is called "the witness of the Spirit." Every Christian has the witness of the Spirit to his sonship. The life of God in the soul is too great and wonderful not to be perceived by the man who has got free from the spirit of the devil. We again say, as we have said often, it is a great experience to be a Christian — to have the divine nature, which means heirship, to have a title to heaven, because we are the children of God and the brethren of Christ. Such a soul with the poet sings : —

> "*Now* I can read my title clear
> To mansions in the skies,
> I'll bid farewell to every fear
> And wipe my weeping eyes."

The days of his mourning are over. An heir of God, he has in his heart the joy of the Holy Ghost.

But as grand and glorious as it is to have a title to heaven, our title may be vitiated if we are not true to our light, as we have seen in the previous chapter. We have no through tickets, with "stop-over privileges," on the road to heaven. If we do not press on with all our power, we shall yet fail, even after we get our title. There are many ways in which men lose estates to which they have a title, if they get in debt, or fail to pay the taxes, or commit certain crimes. So we see that a title may be vitiated in several ways. And right here is a very vital point, because many people say, "Was I not converted? Am I not a child of God? Why should I need anything more?" Here is where many fail in not noting the difference between their *title* to

heaven, and their *fitness* for it.   There is a vast difference between the title that a child has to an estate and
his fitness for it.   Many a child at a very tender age
(many times before he has come to the years of ac-
countability) is an heir to his deceased parents' estate,
but he is far from being fitted for it.   The common law
of the land does not consider any heir fitted for his estate simply because he has a title.   It declares that he
is not fit for it until he be twenty-one years of age, and
even then, if he be an imbecile or insane, he has not the
fitness, but must have a guardian or trustees.   Infants
have a title to heaven by the atonement of Jesus.   But,
nevertheless, they display tempers that are not heavenly, and hence need fitness still.   The qualifications for
fitness are something besides and in addition to the title.
Is it not strange that people cannot see the difference,
but go on saying, "I am a Christian.   I have a title.
That is sufficient"?   *A true Christian will take no chances.
Having a title, he will be tremendously in earnest to get
his fitness.*   Holiness of heart will be no secondary matter to him.   The man who is not greatly anxious about
his fitness takes but little delight or thought about the
inheritance.   We quote a few verses of Scripture here
to substantiate what we have already said.   Paul said to
the Galatians on this point, "The heir, as long as he is
a child, differeth nothing from a servant, though he be
lord of all ; but is under tutors and governors until the
time appointed by his father."   Peter says we are heirs
to an inheritance "reserved in heaven for you who are
kept by the power of God through faith unto salvation."
It is "a kept inheritance for a kept people."   It is
those who are kept — from what ? from the only thing

that can get us off the track — sin. Kept in the only condition that makes us fit for heaven, purity of heart. " Blessed are the pure in heart, for they shall see God." If men who have a title to an earthly estate are careful to keep all the requirements of the law, that they may enter upon it, how can the same men be so careless about the heavenly estate ? how can they be so indifferent about that " holiness without which no man shall see the Lord"? Why is it they will risk their souls where they would not an earthly inheritance ? Jesus said to Nicodemus, "Except a man be born again, he cannot see the kingdom of God." And every man born again does see the kingdom, and does have it set up in his heart. But there is another passage quite as emphatic, "That sanctification without which no man shall see the Lord" (*Revised Version*). A man may see the kingdom by being born again, and then refuse to go on, refuse to get the fitness, and never see the king of that kingdom, for the sight of the king is reserved to the pure in heart. The man who had not on the wedding garment failed to get into the marriage supper. He got into the kingdom, and then failed to get into the marriage supper at last, because he had not on the wedding garment, which is holiness. How can people call themselves Christians, who, in the face of these solemn passages, refuse to seek all the light and grace of holiness possible, refuse to seek the fitness by declaring, "I am converted, I have a title to heaven, that is enough"? Do they not know that good titles are very often lost ? The Israelites lost the Canaan to which they had been called, simply because they would not go in and take possession. When their descendants, forty years later, came up to the land, God told them that it was theirs, just as he did their fathers. The difference between the miserable experience of their fathers and their great prosperity was, they went over and took possession. There are plenty of excuses that people make who do not wish to get the fitness for their inheritance. Some try to mix what God has made clear, and assert that a title is a fitness. If it is, then a good part of the New Testament is meaningless; for it abounds in constant admonitions to the people of God to obtain entire holiness.

CHAPTER VIII.

THE "UP AND DOWN" LIFE.

"Not laying again the foundation of repentance." — HEB. vi. 1.

IF we accept testimony at all, we must believe that there is an "up and down" experience that is supposed by many to be a part of the Christian life. Many good people testify to such an experience, who are honest, and would be believed on any other subject. We slander nobody when we say that such testimonies are heard in the class-meeting as these: "Brethren and sisters, I make a great many crooked paths; pray for me that I may continue on." "I have my ups and downs." The following hymn is in one of the Calvinistic hymnals: —

"A mixture of joy and sorrow,
    I daily do pass through.
Sometimes I'm in the valley,
    And sinking down in woe.

Sometimes I am exalted
    On eagles' wings; I rise
And soar above old Pisgah,
    And almost reach the skies.

Sometimes I go to meeting;
    Sometimes I stay at home;
Sometimes I get a blessing,
    And then I'm glad I come."

This "up and down" experience comes from remaining too long in the initial experiences of grace. God intends that we shall go right on into the Canaan of perfect love; and, as sure as we do not, we shall find it an up and down life. If any one will take a map, and trace the wanderings of the children of Israel, they will find their track was very circuitous, often crossing and re-crossing itself, aimless and purposeless. It resembles very closely "the crooked paths" we hear modern professors of religion speak of, which give to the world such a sorry representation of the Christian life. The apostle gives us a picture of just such a church, in *Heb. v.* and *vi.* It was the church at Jerusalem, who had remained too long in the elementary experience of grace, and had not gone "on to perfection." If we begin with *Heb. v.* 11, we can see the picture, which is a faithful representation of many we meet to-day. He is speaking of Melchisedec thus, "of whom we have many things to say, and hard to be uttered, seeing ye are dull of hearing." There has been a great deal written about Melchisedec, because it is uncertain who he was. Had this church been up to their privileges in the gospel, the church of the ages since might have had this truth revealed to them. But the apostle had to stop because this church was dull of hearing. For thirty years they had been established as a church, and yet they had made little progress; and all the Christian church since then is the loser in knowledge that might have been imparted right here, had this people been up to their privileges. *If we fail to be all that God wants us to be, some one else will suffer as well as ourselves.* It may be our families or friends or neighbors. Let us notice some of the characteristics which the apostle here gives of those who do not go on to perfection.

1. *Dull of hearing.* — This does not mean inability to hear at all, but inability to clearly hear. It makes all the difference in the world as to *what* we are, if we are to hear well. The uncivilized savage who hears first the locomotive whistle in the forest mistakes it for some demon. But civilized man recognizes that it is the token of his nearness to civilization. When the voice came out of heaven, some said "it thundered; others said an angel spake to him." But Jesus recognized the voice of his Father. So when men hear the truth, it depends much upon what they are as to what they will hear. This is the reason there is great responsibility in hearing the gospel. Some congregations are so spiritual they draw the preacher's very best out of his treasury. This moral attitude is the reason so many people find it hard to understand about holiness. They have trifled with the urging of the Spirit to holiness so. much, that their spiritual hearing has become dull. Many a time have we stated that holiness is not a state where we are free from the possibility of falling, only to hear it published abroad that we said we could not sin ; many a time have we declared that we could never arrive at the place where we could not be tempted, only to hear that we have said "we could not be tempted." This is not because people mean to be dishonest, but because they have dulled their spiritual sensibilities by not going on in Christian life.

2. *Dwelling on the first principles of salvation.* — In verse 12 he says, "Ye have need that one teach you

again which be the first principles of the oracles of God." He says in the first part of the verse they ought to have been teachers themselves. Certainly they had, after thirty years of experience. They were ever learning and never coming to a " knowledge of the truth." How many such there are who never can teach any one else, even after long years of professed Christian life. They have to be instructed upon the elements of religion all their life, and cannot comprehend the deeper things of Christian life. In chapter vi. 1, he says, " Leaving the principles of the doctrine of Christ," or as the *R. V.* has it, " Let us cease to speak of the first principles of Christ." All such have to talk of is their conversion. They know nothing of the richer joys that come from more intimate acquaintance with Jesus. The only kind of preaching that feeds them is that which appeals to their sensibilities, — descriptions of death-beds, calling to mind their dead friends and loved ones gone before. And the preacher who succeeds in making them cry without getting them to advance one peg is considered a great man, while they hear unconcernedly those who insist on holiness, — the preparation and fitness for heaven.

3. *Their fondness for, and inability to appreciate any other than, a diet of milk.* — There are three kinds of diet mentioned in the history of the children of Israel. In *Num. xi.* 5 we hear them regretting the Egyptian diet they had left behind them. " We remember the fish which we did eat freely ; the cucumbers, and the melons, and the leeks, and the onions, and the garlick." This represents the worldly enjoyments that the sinner feeds upon. God gave them manna from heaven, and

quails to satisfy them only temporarily, until they got
to Canaan, when they could eat of "the old corn " and
the milk and honey. So now, after we have left the
pleasures of the world, God gives a temporary diet,
called here milk, until we can go on and take "strong
meat." Paul had to feed the church at Corinth on milk,
regretting that they could not endure meat. So here
the Hebrew church had to be fed on the same diet for
thirty years. The meat of the gospel was too much
for their spiritual digestion. There are thousands to-
day who have been in the way as long as this church,
who turn away with loathing from the strong meat of
the gospel. No wonder they are in an up and down
state of experience. Milk is only intended to strengthen
babes just for a brief time, until they are strong enough
to take meat. Strong Christians have to have more
substantial food. God intends regeneration to be temporary until we can go on to get entire sanctification.

4. *Infancy.* — " For he is a babe." Babes make
crooked paths because they have not learned to walk
well, and have not the strength as yet. Babes have a
good many falls. They are up and down. This accounts for so much of the "up and down" life. It is a
sad sight to see a babe after he is thirty years of age,
like this church at Jerusalem. Every household that
has such babes is to be pitied. We pity the minister
who has a church full of them. He has but little time
to do any thing else, because the babes are often fretful.
They quarrel. This is the cause of church quarrels.
The babes do the quarrelling. So Paul said (*see* I
Cor. iii.).

5. *The babes have to be amused.* — To do this takes a

great deal of the time of the church and ministry.
Churches have to be fitted up with reference to amus-
ing the babes.   Revivals have to be put off many times
so as not to interfere with the amusement of the babes.
They are up and down because divided between religion
and amusement.   The amusement craze has struck the
church, called by the name of Jesus, to such an extent
that it is far easier to get the people to the church en-
tertainment than to the social means of grace.   Great
numbers usually may be seen at the former, while at-
tendance is meagre at the latter.   Why is this?   Because people go to that for which they have the most
appetite.   We can tell what people are by what they
like.

6. *Sinning and repenting.* — " Not laying again the
foundation of repentance."   It will be seen, then, by
this that repentance is the foundation of the Christian
life.   He who commits sin destroys his spiritual life.
" The soul that sinneth it shall die."   And yet so com-
pletely has the devil captured modern theology that it
is thought that we can commit sin and yet be the children of God.   So multitudes are sinning and repenting
all their lives.   This is their idea of religion.   They
spend their time tearing down and relaying the foundation.   They get no time for building the superstructure
upon the foundation.   The true way to save a foundation is to place a house upon it.   The true way to retain the experience of justification is to go on to entire
sanctification, and let entire sanctification preserve our
justification, just as a building by its very existence pre-
serves its foundation.   We have known of people laying the foundation of a house, and, before they get

ready to put the house on it, the foundation had so crumbled that it had to be relaid. There are thousands who are doing the same thing in their spiritual life. The true way to keep from backsliding is to keep pressing on in spiritual life. And hence we find hosts of people whose Christian life is simply an effort at self-preservation. Our churches become, not life-saving stations, but hospitals. The true cure for this up and down state is getting rid of the inward tendency which keeps us back, and makes it difficult to advance.

7. *The tendency to doubt.* — " And of faith." Faith and repentance always go together. So true is this that there has been dispute as to which is first in the Christian life. Neither is first. Repentance is named first, but it is impossible to repent in the fullest sense without faith ; and it is impossible to exercise saving faith without having repented. This tendency to doubt, in the experience of one who knows he has been saved, is remarkable, and yet it is a fact. There is an under-current leading to rank unbelief in the experience of those who are as certain of their conversion as of their existence. This tendency weakens religious experience, and hinders them from advancing to the highlands of Christian experience. It leads them to fear that lions may be in the way. It makes them cowards instead of brave explorers. When a person begins to be swayed by this tendency to doubt, he soon refuses to go on. He listens to his fears ; he looks at circumstances and surroundings ; he looks at things from the worldly standpoint of numbers and worldly resources, instead of looking to God and his promises. This was the trouble with Israel when they came to the borders of

the promised land. They got scared at the report of
the false spies, who told them of the walled cities and
giants in the land of Canaan, instead of trusting in
God, who told them to go on and possess the land. So
many to-day listen to accounts of fanaticism, or of fail-
ures, or inconsistencies, or the weakness of human nature, or of ridicule and opposition. These things are
more congenial to their hearts than trusting in God.
The apostle in the third chapter of Hebrews holds this
people up as an example to us, saying, " Take heed,
brethren, lest there be in any of you an evil heart of
unbelief, in departing from the living God." In the
tenth chapter he tells us that at this stage of Christian
life the definition of faith is *going ahead*, " Now the
just shall live by faith : but if any man draw back, my
soul hath no pleasure in him. Now we are not of those
who draw back unto perdition, but of those that believe." The great cause of backsliding is " an evil
heart of unbelief." Dr. Adam Clarke says on this
point, " A slothful heart sees dangers, lions and giants,
everywhere ; and therefore refuses to proceed in the
heavenly path. Many of the *spies* contribute to this
by the bad reports they bring of the heavenly country.
Certain preachers allow 'that the land is good, that it
flows with milk and honey,' and go so far as to show
some of its fruits ; but they discourage the people by
stating the impossibility of overcoming their enemies.
' Sin,' say they, ' cannot be destroyed in this life — it
will always dwell in you — the Anakim cannot be
conquered — we are but as grasshoppers against the
Anakim,' etc. Here and there a Joshua and a Caleb,
trusting alone in the infinite efficacy of that blood

which cleanses from all unrighteousness, boldly stand forth and say, 'Their defence is departed from them, and the Lord is with us; let us go up at once and possess the land, for we are able to overcome.' We can do all things through Christ strengthening us; he will purify us unto himself, and give us that rest from sin here which his death has procured and his word promised. Reader, canst thou not take God at his word? He has never yet failed thee! Surely, then, thou hast no reason to doubt. Thou hast never tried him to the uttermost." That is the point exactly. Many doubt the Lord without any good reason for so doing. There is need of, and, thank God! there is, a better experience than the "up and down" life of which we have been speaking. We can leave the foundations. As sure as we do not we shall be weak Christians all our days. We can go on to that perfection of Christian life which is free from doubt, because free from sin, — a perfect faith. We can arrive at the place where we can say with Faber. —

> " I know not what it is to doubt;
>   My heart is always gay;
> I run no risk, for come what will,
>   God always has his way."

Some are scared at this word "Perfection;" but it is a Bible term, and whatever else it may mean, it means freedom from the "up and down" life of which we have just been speaking. Reader, the cause of the up and down life is sin in the heart, which, like a loadstone, pulls downward towards hell. Get rid of the weight, and then the whole course of life will be up, with no "downs" of sinning against God.

CHAPTER IX.

THE MORE ABUNDANT LIFE.

" That they might have life, and that they might have it more abundantly."
JOHN x. 10.

We have seen that a Christian is one who is a possessor of the divine life. There are degrees of divine life just as truly in the spiritual as in the natural world. Some people object to anything more than regeneration. But there are hindrances to regeneration that impair spiritual health. A sick man has life, but not abundant life. A child is born of leprous parents, and for a time bids fair to defeat the inherited tendencies of leprosy. He is as well formed and developed and as fair as any other child, but in time the inner law of leprosy manifests itself. His future life is a constant struggle against disease. He has life, but not that abundant life that characterizes those born with pure blood ("the blood is the life"). Many will admit this in the natural world who deny the corresponding experience in the spiritual life. There are inherited tendencies that we have to struggle against in the spiritual life as truly as some do in the natural life. All mankind inherit a predisposition to sin, just as some children inherit a predisposition to alcohol or tobacco, or inherit the seeds of disease. "Adam begat a son in his own likeness" after he fell from the image of God in which he had been created. The universal testimony of the church in all its branches is, that these tendencies to sin do remain in them that are regenerate. As poison in the system is a hindrance to health of body, so is sin a hindrance to the spiritual life. Many of God's dear children are thus dwarfed and stunted in their spiritual development, as we wish to show still farther. We note some of the manifestations of experience that show the need of more abundant spiritual life.

1. *Fickle appetite.* — Poison in the system, or poor health from any cause, is often evinced by a fickle appetite. Often it is weak and then again abnormally strong. We see the same thing in the appetite for spiritual things in those who have inbred sin. At times there is a great love for the word of God and prayer; at other times appetite for these things is weak. There is too much of this spasmodic, fitful appetite in the church to-day. Take all the poison out of the system, and appetite increases and is a sign of perfect health. Such people have to have preaching spiced up with a great deal of the pathetic; often the preaching which can cause the most weeping is considered the gospel, when there is no thought in it all of a holy life, while those preachers who touch and rouse the conscience are considered austere and are unpopular.

2. *An intermittent state.* — When malarial poison gets into the system, there is an intermittent life. First the patient is in a fever, then he is shaking with ague. When the poison is eliminated, then these phenomena cease. This is the cause of the revival heat and the reaction that follows again and again. This gives birth

to the sentiment that has found expression in song
thus, —

"Why are my winters so long?"

Get sin out of the heart, and there is a constant glow of
love and zeal for God.   This is the reason that holiness
makes a one-idea man of him who gets it.   At last perpetual motion has been discovered.   It puts tireless
energy in the soul.

3. *A struggle for existence.* — There are thousands of
sufferers from disease who are making a fight for life.
This battle takes all their time and strength.   They
have no time to help others, but quite often others have
to help them.   And there are thousands in the church
who have a hard time in retaining spiritual life.   They
have no time to help others.   Their efforts are spent
in keeping alive.   Sometimes they ask their spiritual
advisers for advice.   They are often told that the way
to get strong is by helping others.   But this advice is
like telling a man struggling against drowning to save
others.   Men do not become strong by work, but by
what they eat.   And men cannot eat to any profit without appetite, and appetite for spiritual things is poor
when the poison of sin is still in the heart.   The church
has been a hospital too long.   Too long has it been
adjusting itself to the popular hymn, —

"Hold the fort, for I am coming;
Jesus signals still."

Too long this defensive warfare has been waged,
instead of an aggressive campaign against the devil.
Paul says, "The weapons of our warfare are not carnal,

but mighty through God to the pulling down of strong-holds." It is time this were better understood. Zion is called to aggressive warfare. Every Christian is called to do something else than fight his own lusts, evil desires, and sin. He ought to go forth as a warrior against sin. The church will never take the place her Lord designed until she gets on the aggressive. Every church ought to be an arsenal from which, seven days in the week, her hosts all equipped should go forth to make trouble for the devil, and shake his kingdom. Never can she do this while maintaining the contest against her own self and selfishness. When the church gets the victory over self, then she will be ready to shake the kingdom of hell. To compare the modern church, with its lack of power to convict men, or to stop the abuses that cry to heaven in modern society, with the description of her in the Bible, would excite ridicule. To compare the self-pampering, worldly religion of to-day with the picture of her "coming up out of the wilderness, leaning on the arm of her beloved," "clear as the sun, fair as the moon, terrible as an army with banners," would be a farce. We once saw on the walls of a church a picture of a woman clinging to a cross. About her were dashing waves and the fragments of the wreck from which she had been cast. She was clinging for dear life to that cross, lest the angry waves should wash her away. The picture illustrated the current idea of religion. What a toilsome task was hers. A thousand times we have thought of it, and wondered how long her strength would last. She was putting forth all her strength for self-preservation. She had no time nor strength to help others. What a pic-

ture! If we were a painter, we would like to paint
another picture. We would place her at the foot of the
cross, safe from the waves, and with a hand stretched
out to help others to escape from the waves of sin. We
would name the picture, *Resting at the Cross.* This
rest of activity — rest as regards our own salvation and
activity to save the world — can be obtained only by
a fully saved church. The Christian who has yet to
struggle with himself cannot be at his best for the
salvation of others, or for pulling down the kingdom
of Satan. We hear sometimes some dear old brother
declare, " I was converted years ago, and I am still converted. I am yet alive." As if it were remarkable that
he had managed to keep alive. Abundant life is the
condition of being at our best, both for God and humanity.

4. *Sin in the heart causes an enfeebled condition of
life.* — We hear much about "crooked paths." These
come from an enfeebled condition. It requires health
and strength to continue in a straightforward course.
This is the reason we hear some say, "I am serving the
Lord in my poor weak way." The divine way is to be
strong, and serve him with a perfect heart. And the
sooner people serve him in *his* way, and not in their
"poor weak way," the better for them. Lazarus is a
type of the difference between these two degrees of
life. He had life when he came out of the tomb, but
he was still bound by the garb of death. Jesus said,
" Loose him and let him go." So now he says of those
alive from the dead, but yet hindered by "the remains"
of their former condition, " Loose them and let them
go." When the church gets the Pentecostal gift of

divine power, then and only then will it come to that condition prophesied, where " One shall chase a thousand, and two put ten thousand to flight."

5. *A state of debility is a state of more or less misery.* — We have known people who had life enough to become the basis for suffering at times, because of the inroads of disease. And we have heard people declare that they had just religion enough to make them miserable. We suppose by the latter state they meant that in their desire to serve God they became legal in their service, and were constantly in fear lest they had left something undone, or had done something they ought not. This is the service of which Paul speaks in Galatians, performed by those who act more like servants than children. A man may have just enough of this kind of religion to make him miserable. And this is the reason so many say they have just enough religion to make them miserable. There is something better for God's children — abundant life. Abundant life is joyous life ; and it makes life a pleasure, not a burden. We have often thought, as we looked upon a congregation, suppose the bodies of these people were like their souls, what a deplorable condition they would find themselves in. Some would be gasping for breath. Others would be walking on crutches ; others would be writhing in agony ; while others would be carried to the tomb. *Abundant life is the best condition for growth.* A sickly child develops very slowly, if at all. Disease hinders growth. While it is true that a Christian grows somewhat before sin is removed from his heart, yet he can never develop so rapidly or symmetrically as after the sin is removed. This is the reason the Bible usually speaks of growth

in grace after it has spoken of the purification of the heart. Sin, like disease in the body, is the great hindrance to growth in grace. God wants to entirely sanctify his church, in order that they may develop properly in this world ; just as the farmer kills the weeds to help the growth of the corn, but never grows corn in order to kill weeds. The latter process would be as absurd as the attempts people are making to outgrow sin. There is no analogy in nature nor teaching in the Bible for outgrowing sin. Jesus gives us an illustration of this in the parable of the sower. The third class were those where the seed springs up in thorny ground. The thorns and briers sprang up with the good seed and choked it, so that it brought forth " no fruit to perfection." The fruit was imperfect because much of the strength and nourishment of the soil went into the thorns, when it should have been taken up by the good seed. On the other hand, the good ground hearers were those whose hearts was free from these hindrances, and brought forth abundant fruit, " some an hundred fold, some sixty fold, some thirty fold."

This thought of abundant life is considered by some to be fanaticism. But why should it be considered fanaticism to have a healthy soul, any more than to have a healthy body ? Is not God as able to give one as the other ? and is he not willing ? Does he like to have sickly children ? Is it any credit to him to have sin, the work of the enemy, in his children ? Does it represent fairly the salvation of our God to have it understood that his salvation does not save fully ? It seems to us it glorifies Satan more than Jesus, to declare that Jesus cannot, or will not, save us from sin. When the

Word of God declares that he "cannot look upon sin with the least degree of allowance," will he yet allow it in his children? Whatever good is in man is in spite of the wishes and protest of the devil. And must we say that whatever sin is in us is permitted by him who hates sin? Must his children have that in them that he abhors above all things else? If it be fanaticism to prefer a healthy soul, then we are deluded by the plain teachings of the Bible. This cry of "fanaticism" has always originated from those who are in the rear of the army. Since the days when Joseph saw more than his brethren, this cry has arisen from those in the rear, who have cast stones at the pioneers who are in the vanguard. Joseph's brethren called him the "dreamer," and treated him accordingly. But the dreamer knew what he was about, and the time came when the brethren found it out. Ask the grass that springs in the meadow, "What is life?" and if it had a voice, it might reply, "It is above the mere existence of the mineral kingdom." It is to have that mysterious power that enables one to grow, and increase, and develop. Go a step higher, and ask the ox that crops the grass, "What is life?" and if he could speak, doubtless he would declare his superiority to the plant-life — to the grass which he eats. A step higher than the animal brings us to man, gifted beyond the beasts in intelligence, reason, imagination, and discretion. It is not fanaticism to declare that man has a form of life that the animal creation knows nothing of. If we go a step higher, into the spiritual kingdom, we shall discover that the spiritual man lives in a realm, and is possessed of a life, of which the natural man is absolutely ignorant. And

it is no more fanatical to profess the life that is hid with
Christ in God, which all true Christians enjoy, than it
would be for the grass in the vegetable kingdom to profess a life unknown to the mineral, or for the ox to
profess a life that the plant is ignorant of. If we go a
step higher we shall come to the degree of spiritual life
that may be called life more abundant ; and why should
it be considered fanatical, any more than to look upon
the other states of existence as fanaticism ?

There is nothing needed more to-day than a church
with abundant life. No other people are competent to
solve the great questions of the day, and correct the
crying evils of society. No other can exemplify the
golden rule, or carry out the love that not only "worketh no ill to its neighbor," but loves its neighbor as
itself.

CHAPTER X.

CHRISTIAN PRIESTHOOD.

"A royal priesthood." — 1 PET. ii. 9.

THE Christian is a priest. Under the Old Dispensation the priest had a double office. He had a relation both to God and to man. He was a mediator between the two. When he stood in the presence of God, he represented the people. When he stood in the presence of the people, he represented God. Thus he had his manward and his Godward relations. "Every high priest," says Paul the Apostle, "taken from among men is ordained for men in things pertaining to God, that he may offer both gifts and sacrifice for sins" (*Heb. v.* 1). On the Godward side we find the priesthood as far back as the days of Noah. He stood up for God, and interceded with a wicked world, seeking to persuade them to forsake their sins. He offered sacrifice to God when the eight came forth in safety from the ark. Abraham, too, exercised the priestly office — not only when he made the sacrifice of the animals at the time of his own justification (see *Gen. xv.* 9), but also when guilty Sodom was doomed by divine wrath, we hear him pleading that it be spared if ten righteous persons could be found. And his prayer was granted. Job was also a priest to intercede with God for men. After his mistaken and unsympathetic friends had been re-

buked for their hard speeches, God commanded them
to bring their sacrifices, "and my servant Job shall pray
for you, for him will I accept." Moses, too, stood in
the gap between an offended God and a backslidden
church, and cried, "Yet now, if thou wilt forgive their
sin — ; and if not, blot me, I pray thee, out of thy book
which thou hast written." Paul said, "Brethren, my
heart's desire and prayer to God for Israel is, that they
might be saved." He also impresses upon Timothy,
as a young preacher, the importance of the duty of intercession for all men. "I exhort therefore, that, first of
all, supplications, prayers, intercessions, and giving of
thanks, be made for all men." He closes this injunction by saying, " for this is good and acceptable in the
sight of God our Saviour ; who will have all men to be
saved, and to come unto the knowledge of the truth."
Jesus declared to his Father of his followers, " As thou
hast sent me into the world, even so have I also sent
them into world." When we remember that Jesus was
sent into the world to sacrifice himself for the world, to
be its light, and to be a mediator between God and man,
we see clearly that the Christian is the world's hope.
A part of the perfect Christian nature as well as duty
is the expression of perfect love to men. When sin is
cleansed from the heart, then selfishness departs. He
lives to spend his life for the good of men. He sacrifices for them as Jesus did. There is never any difficulty in getting sinners saved where there is a band of
such Christians. Their prayers and intercession with
God and their sacrifices for men bring down convicting
power upon the unsaved. The query is sometimes
raised, " Why does not conviction rest upon the unsaved

as in former days?" May not one answer be that
there are so few that wrestle and intercede with God
for the unsaved. There is so little travail of soul.
It requires unselfishness to produce travail of soul. Holiness of heart begets unselfishness. No wonder that
great observer of Christian experience, John Wesley,
said of the preaching of holiness, "Wherever it is
preached revivals usually prevail."

But there is another aspect of the responsibility and
necessity of this kind of character in society. We live
in an age that, like all others, has its peculiarities. We
live in a time when great problems are demanding solu-
tion. Great issues are at stake. If society is to remain stable, there are great wrongs to be righted, great
crimes that are being perpetrated upon society, and
monstrous iniquities that cry to heaven for redress.
The times may well call for the imprecation of St.
James, "Go to now, ye rich men, weep and howl for
your miseries that are heaped upon you." "Behold the
hire of the laborers who have reaped down your fields,
which is of you kept back by fraud, crieth ; and the
cries of them which have reaped are entered into the
ears of the Lord of sabaoth." There is a great struggle
between capital and labor, which grows fiercer ; there is
a social evil that grows more unblushing as it drags its
thousands of innocents from virtue to a living death
and the blackness of eternal despair. Intemperance
like a vampire is sucking the life-blood of the nations.
A perverted type of optimism closes its eyes, and refuses
to recognize these glaring, increasing evils. Where are
the priests like Abraham who shall stand between God
and Sodom to plead for it ? Where are the good Samar-

itans that shall sacrifice for the bruised and wounded?
Where are the men that shall be illustrations of honesty
in this age of fraud? Where are the Elijahs who shall
call down fire from heaven, and destroy the priests of
Baal? Where is the salt that shall preserve the putrefy-
ing mass of society? Where is the light for the world's
darkness? Where are the representatives of him who
died on the cross for a guilty, wretched, suffering world?
Where are those ready to sacrifice to bring the world to
the foot of that cross? It is the fully sanctified, or
there is no hope for this world. Such are the peculiar
conditions of society to-day, that we must, as a church,
make an advance. We cannot be satisfied with the old
line of battle. We must push out against the forces of
evil that are so blatant and defiant to-day. *There must
be a more intense Christianity, or the victory must be given
to the enemy.* We must go farther even than the golden
rule. We must do as Jesus did,— sacrifice ourselves for
the good of humanity. In fact, the Salvation Army are
doing this in their slum work, their prison brigades,
their rescue homes, their self-denial, their hand-to-hand
work; but this is not enough. We must have a sanctified church that will reorganize society on the basis
of equal rights. We must have Christian corporations
with souls. We must raise up in this age of conscience-
less competition an enlightened Christian conscience.
Some one must lead the van by self-sacrifice. This is
the only hope. Multitudes are looking, sometimes in
despair, at the Christian church, the divine mediator, to
set the example, and exhibit the great law of self-sacrifice in bringing about the great reform for which society
is voicing its righteous petition. There never was

more need of a practical sanctification than to-day. And unless nominal Christianity shall refurnish itself with the savor which it has to some extent lost, then God will allow it to be trodden under foot of men, and furnish a better Christianity to take its place. The really sanctified Christian will not only live to enjoy himself, but be the world's representative, showing by his self-sacrifice that he possesses the heart of the Master who was the lover of mankind. As sure as Wesleyanism saved society in the last century, so sure God must have a sanctified people to save society to-day, or there is no hope.

On the other hand, the Christian is the representative of God also. The only visible representative of God on earth is the Christian. It is amazing that man should be allowed to take this place. But it is nevertheless true, that the weakest child of God occupies a position that has been denied to the angels. These are the branches of the true Vine. We know that a vine bears its fruit on its branches, and not on the trunk. And since Jesus went to heaven, there is no one to bear the fruits of godliness and reflect the divine glory except men, — those who have been redeemed, washed, and translated out of the kingdom of darkness. These are the lights of the world, reflecting the glory of God.

In a partial sense the creation reflects the glory of God, as far as his creative and preserving character is concerned. But in a higher sense the true Christian reflects God, for he is the product of the power that saves and keeps from sin. This expression of God's power cannot be found in all the works of God in nature. As the poet says, —

" 'Twas great to speak a world from naught,
    'Tis greater to redeem."

A sinner is a representative of Satan. A Christian represents God. The one shows what Satan can do, the other is an exponent of the power of God ; the one is a sample of the enemy's work, the other is a sample of the power of God. There are those religionists who allow great power to Satan, but with strange inconsistency deny equal power to Jesus. They allow the power of Satan in his work of the ruin of the human soul, but deny the power of Jesus Christ to perfectly restore the ruin that sin has made in the human soul. They acknowledge that Satan can make perfect sinners, but deny that Jesus can make perfect saints. They believe that Satan was manifest to destroy the work of God, and that he is a success in this direction in a multitude of instances. But they deny the inspired Scripture that declares that Jesus "was manifested to destroy the works of the devil."

To all such we lay down this proposition, involved in the priesthood of the Christian, namely ; *The Christian is the only visible divine representative in the world to-day.* He is a sample of the saving power of the gospel of the Son of God. We are commanded to "Let your light so shine before men, that they may see your good works, and glorify your Father which is in heaven." This being true, if God does not save his people *from* their sins, it is a confession of the failure of the gospel ; it is an untruthful representation of the holy God. A patient wasting away with disease is a poor representative of the skill of his doctor. Were we compelled to believe that Jesus Christ cannot save from sin, we would believe the Christian to be a representative of Satan rather than of a holy God.

If we found the trade-mark of a manufacturing company upon shoddy that passed for high-grade fabric, we should be compelled to consider the whole business a humbug. What shall we say, then, at finding the divine trade-mark upon sin? What shall we say at finding the name Christian upon a sinful man? What shall we say of a holy God being represented by those who not only are not saved from sin, but who even deny the possibility of such a salvation? If, in buying the article, we were told it was high grade, and properly represented the skill and honor of the firm, when all the time we could see that it was only shoddy; and if, when we called attention to the fact, we were told that it was an attempt at good quality, and that it was better to attempt even if one failed than to make no attempt at all, — what would we think? And yet that is the way men talk of the practical workings of the atonement of Him "who gave himself for us, that he might redeem us from all iniquity, and purify unto himself a peculiar people, zealous of good works." If the medicine does not cure the patient, then the disease is more than a match for the medicine. The divine representative must be like the God he represents, or he is not his representative on earth. No man can represent God unless he is holy, for God is holy. Hence we are told "as he is, so are we in this world." Unholy people represent the devil, and not God. And if unholy people bear the trade-mark *Christian*, then they have committed the crime of stealing the divine trade-mark to put the devil's goods upon the market, and hinder the work of God. The proposition is true, then, that only holy people represent God, and all others represent the devil and his power. The Christian priesthood, then, is a high calling. It is patterned after the Jewish priesthood ; from that priesthood sprang the idea of priesthood and its twofold office of intercession for man before God and representation of God before man. We note the following points of similarity.

1. *Priests are born to the priesthood.* — No one could be a priest under the ancient ritual unless one were of the house of Aaron. It came by birth. And as we have seen in previous chapters, no one can be a priest in the succession of Jesus Christ unless he be born into the divine family by the new birth. Thus God becomes his Father, and Jesus Christ his elder brother.

2. Notwithstanding a priest must be born in the family of Levi, yet even then he had to be *consecrated to the priesthood.* This was a special and definite act after his birth. His birth entitled him to the office, but he was not fitted for its duties until he had been consecrated. Many born to the Christian priesthood do not see this; and many more, we fear, pretend not to see it. They say they were consecrated to the priesthood when born. But this is a mistake. Consecration to the priesthood always takes place after birth. This is always the order, — birth, then sanctification. Jesus, our forerunner and example, a high priest "after the order of Melchisedec," was not consecrated and anointed by the Holy Spirit for his priesthood until thirty years of age. Every analogy, therefore, shows that we are first born priests by the new birth, then by an act of consecration we become priests after our conversion.

There are thousands called Christians who exercise no functions of the spiritual priesthood, have no real intercession before God and man, but labor to keep an existence, because they do not consecrate themselves entirely to God. We note some farther points of analogy between the consecration of priests under the Old and New Dispensations.

1. *The priest was washed.* — "Aaron and his sons thou shalt bring to the door of the tabernacle of the congregation, and shalt wash them with water" (*Ex. xxix.* 4). They must be "clean that bear the vessels of the Lord." God wants clean priests to-day. We cannot fully exercise the Christian functions God has called us to unless we are clean. We must be cleansed, just as Aaron's sons were, *after we are born into* this "kingdom of priests."

2. They were then clothed with "the holy garments." God himself selected these garments. The consecrated believer is clothed with the garments of holiness after being cleansed. The removal of sin is the negative side of entire sanctification, and the putting on of righteousness is the positive side. It is the double experience of the putting off of "the old man," and the putting on of "the new man which after God is created in righteousness and true holiness."

3. *Anointing.* — Having been cleansed and clothed, the priest was then anointed with the holy anointing oil, typical of the anointing of the Holy Spirit to-day. These three ceremonies took place at the same time, cleansing, clothing, and anointing, showing us that there is no special third experience. These three take place at the same time, just as justification, regeneration, and adoption are synchronous.

Reader, you are called to be a son of God of the true tribe of Levi. If you have made your calling and election sure, you have a still higher call. God calls thee to the priesthood. Thou wert converted in order to enter the priesthood. Stop not with being a son, go on to the priest-hood. Priests of old forfeited their divine right by dis-obedience, and died, and many to-day are doing the same.

The world all about is dying for lack of this minis-try. Only the anointed priesthood can ever success-fully avail in intercession for a lost world. "If I regard iniquity in my heart, the Lord will not hear me." Only a consecrated, anointed priesthood can truly represent our great High Priest in this world, among his foes. "Ye are a chosen generation, a royal priesthood, an holy nation, a peculiar people; that ye should show forth the praises [virtues] of him who hath called you out of darkness into his marvellous light."

Only the fully consecrated Christian priesthood is fit for heaven. "Holiness, without which no man shall see the Lord."

Our High Priest is now before the throne making intercession for us; if he brings us safely home, it will be because we consent to be fully consecrated and anointed to the priesthood. And then we can rejoice in the language of the redeemed, "Unto him that loved us, and washed us in his own precious blood, and hath made us kings and priests to God and his Father; to him be glory and dominion for ever and ever. Amen." Reader, if this book shall have been the means of establishing you in the Christian priest-hood as a fit intercessor with God for men, and a fit representative of his saving power, our object in writ-ing it will be met. *Amen.*

CHAPTER XI.

HOLINESS.

" Holiness, without which no man shall see the Lord." — HEB. xii 14.

A RELIGION not in harmony with common sense could not have come from the God of the Bible. God is the author of common sense, and also of true religion ; and these, like all his works, never conflict. It having been revealed by God that this life is a preface to the life to come, it is in accord with good sense that we must get our fitness for that life while in this world. There used to be a kind of preaching that asserted that every soul went to heaven at death, regardless of character. But this was so revolting to common sense, that a sinner could go immediately to dwell with a holy God and angels, that the position was given up. Old-fashioned Universalism is dead, and no one preaches it. Instead of that, modern Universalists preach what is called " Restorationism." By this is meant that a preparation is needed for heaven after we die. This is somewhat akin to the doctrine of purgatory as taught by the Roman Catholic Church. All admit that to dwell in heaven we must have the fitness. We wish to lay down a few propositions that we believe are in harmony with common sense, and see if they are also in harmony with the Bible.

I. Whatever is essential to our fitness for heaven

ought to be found in the Bible as a plain declaration. It ought not to be found in one or two obscure places, but constantly, plainly, and emphatically. For, if the Bible contains the true religion, it certainly ought to tell us plainly what God expects of us as a qualification to live with him.

II. Whatever is necessary to fit us for heaven ought to be the chief theme of the preachers. To preach anything that does not bear upon this, the fitness for heaven, or not to preach in such a way that all may know what it is and how to obtain it and retain it, is doing the people a cruel wrong which is irremediable. The preachers are in the world to urge upon the people the fitness for heaven. If not, what are they for?

III. Whatever is necessary to fit us for heaven ought to be the specialty of everybody. We ought to think of nothing else or talk of nothing else until we have got to the place where we are ready to go to heaven at a moment's notice. And having obtained that fitness, we certainly ought to make it the special theme of our lives, lest we lose it, and in order that other people also may obtain it. We shall have little time for anything else except those things necessary to keep soul and body together properly until we are sent for, to go to that place which our preparation entitles us to.

IV. Whatever is essential to fit us for heaven ought to be possessed by us each moment. We could not afford to be without it a single moment, for that might be the very moment that we were called to exchange worlds. It is poor management to let insurance run out for a single day. Many people have been ruined at just this point. Whatever fits us for heaven is too precious for us to be without a single moment. We ought to keep insured all the time, or insurance amounts to nothing.

V. Whatever is necessary to fit us for heaven ought to be within the grasp of all people, without regard to age, size, color, gifts, education, or sex, otherwise God would be neither merciful nor just.

VI. Whatever is necessary to fit us for heaven ought to comprise and embrace all the duties and details of life in one sum. If the preacher had to preach on all details of life, one by one, a great many people would be dead before he had got through the list. We need, then, something that will strike the centre of the circumference of life's duties at once, and radiate out into all its details. We believe these propositions will commend themselves to the judgment of every candid man. We wish now to try them by Scripture, and see if the Word of God sustains them. Does the Word of God declare plainly, constantly, and emphatically, the essential for heaven ? Is it in one or two passages, or throughout the book ? The answer is direct and unhesitating. The Word declares " HOLINESS, WITHOUT WHICH NO MAN SHALL SEE THE LORD."

We notice that this is the teaching of the Bible everywhere. It starts with a holy pair, who, having a free will, fell into sin. The plan of salvation was given to restore the race to the state from which they fell. We find that Enoch walked with God, which he certainly could not have done, had he not been himself holy ; for " how can two walk together except they be agreed." Noah "was a perfect man in all his generations." Abraham obeyed the divine command to " Walk before me,

and be thou perfect." Jacob declared on his death-
bed that the angel at Peniel " redeemed me from all
evil." He assured Jacob of this by changing his name,
which meant a change to holy character. When God
led Israel out of Egypt, he brought them up to Mt.
Sinai, and assured them that, if they would keep. his
commandments, he would make them a holy people
(*Ex. xix.* 6). That law which they promised to keep
was the law of perfect love to God and man. Jesus
said it embraced our whole duty. Paul says, " Wherefore the law is holy, and the commandment holy, and
just, and good." At Mt. Sinai God gave them the ritual of worship that taught holiness in typical form.
The cleansing of the leper, the scape-goat, the depart-
ments of the tabernacle, the dress of the high priest,
the priesthood and all its functions, all typified holiness.
God commanded the Israelites, " Be ye holy," again
and again. He declared, "Thou shalt be perfect with
the Lord thy God." We hear David praying, "Create
in me a clean heart, O God." We hear him declaring,
" Mark the perfect man, and behold the upright : for the
end of that man is peace." Again we hear him say,
" Truly God is good to Israel, even to such as are of
a clean heart." And again, "Blessed are the undefiled in the way." We read in *Isa. vi.* that that
prophet received an experience whereby his iniquity
was purged, and his sin taken away. God said to Israel,
" And I will turn my hand upon thee, and purely purge
away thy dross, and take away all thy tin." Through
the mouth of Zechariah he says, " In that day there
shall be a fountain opened to the house of David for
sin and for uncleanness." This is often quoted as if it

were in the church there is a fountain opened for the unconverted; but it reads, "to the house of David." Malachi says of the work of the Holy Spirit, "He shall sit as a refiner and purifier of silver," and again, "He is like a refiner's fire."

We have given a few of the many passages that show the trend of the Old Testament. We now turn to the New Testament. We give a few passages here, which we cannot stop to comment upon. The first chapter of Matthew declares by the mouth of the angel Gabriel, "Thou shalt call his name Jesus, because he shall save his people from their sins." Zacharias, filled with the Holy Ghost, in *Luke i.* declares that Jesus came that, "We being delivered out of the hand of our enemies might serve him without fear, in holiness and righteousness before him, all the days of our life." In his first sermon Jesus said, "Blessed are the pure in heart, for they shall see God," and "Be ye therefore perfect, even as your Father which is in heaven is perfect." He declared of the branches of the vine (true Christians), "Every branch in me that beareth fruit he purgeth it, that it may bring forth more fruit." He could not go to Gethsemane and Calvary until he had prayed for the men who had been preaching for him, "Sanctify them through thy truth: thy word is truth." Peter declares that, by the Pentecostal baptism, the disciples had their hearts purified by faith (*Acts xv.* 9). Paul bids farewell to the elders of the Ephesian church and says, "I commend you to God, and the word of his grace, which is able to build you up, and to give you an inheritance among all them that are sanctified." When Paul was on trial before King Agrippa, he declared that Jesus at the

time of his conversion gave him his commission to get
men saved, in these words, "That they may receive
forgiveness of sins, and inheritance among them which
are sanctified by faith that is in me" (*Acts xxvi.* 18).

The epistles of Paul are full of this idea.   If exhortations to holiness are taken out of the epistles, there
would not be much left ; for this is what they were
written for.   To the Romans he says, "Our old man
is crucified with him, that the body of sin might be
destroyed, that henceforth we should not serve sin."
"How shall we that are dead to sin live any longer
therein ? "   And again, " I beseech you therefore, brethren, by the mercies of God, that ye present your bodies a
living sacrifice, holy, acceptable unto God, which is your
reasonable service.   And be not conformed to this
world ; but be ye transformed by the renewing of your
mind, that ye may prove what is that good, and acceptable, and perfect will of God."   To the Corinthians he
writes, " Having therefore these promises, dearly beloved, let us cleanse ourselves from all filthiness of the
flesh and spirit, perfecting holiness in the fear of God."
He closes his second epistle by saying, " Be perfect."
To the Galatians he says, " I am crucified with Christ :
nevertheless I live ; yet not I, but Christ liveth in me :
and the life I now live I live by the faith of the Son
of God."   To the Ephesians he says more on this
subject than we can quote.   We give a part of it.
" According as he hath chosen us in him before the
foundation of the world, that we should be holy and
without blame before him in love."   This is good "election doctrine."   "Christ also loved the church, and gave
himself for it ; that he might sanctify it by the washing

of water by the word, that he might present it to himself a glorious church, not having spot, or wrinkle, or any such thing; but that it should be holy and without blemish." To the Colossians he writes, declaring that Christ died "to present you holy and unblamable and unreprovable in his sight." He tells the Thessalonians that "God hath not called us unto uncleanness, but unto holiness." "This is the will of God, even your sanctification." He closes his epistle by saying, "The very God of peace sanctify you wholly; and I pray God your whole spirit and soul and body be preserved blameless unto the coming of our Lord Jesus Christ. Faithful is he that calleth you, who also will do it." To Timothy he says, "Now the end of the commandment is love out of a pure heart, and of a good conscience, and of faith unfeigned." To Titus he states the object of the atonement to be to "redeem us from all iniquity, and purify unto himself a peculiar people, zealous of good works."

The inspired author of Hebrews gives an epistle that is saturated with holiness. We give only a few passages. "Wherefore he is able also to save them to the uttermost that come unto God by him, seeing he ever liveth to make intercession for them." "For by one offering he hath perfected them that are sanctified, whereof the Holy Ghost is a witness to us." "Holiness, without which no man shall see the Lord." "Wherefore Jesus also, that he might sanctify the people with his own blood, suffered without the gate." The apostle James also states the question thus, "Cleanse your hands, ye sinners; and purify your hearts, ye double-minded." Peter says a great deal more than we have space to give.

Here are some of his sayings: "Through sanctification
of the Spirit." "As he which hath called you is holy,
so be ye holy in all manner of conversation; because
it is written, Be ye holy; for I am holy." The apostle
John writes, "The blood of Jesus Christ his Son
cleanseth us from all sin." Jude wrote only a short
epistle; but it is in it, thus: "Sanctified by God the
Father, and preserved in Jesus Christ." John in his
apocalyptic vision heard one of the elders say of that
great host in heaven, "These are they which came
out of great tribulation, and have washed their robes,
and made them white in the blood of the Lamb. *Therefore* are they before the throne of God, and serve him
day and night in his temple."

We think we have shown from Scripture that holiness, the requirement of and for heaven, is all through
the Bible. We have been able only to quote a few passages. Let us see if the second proposition is equally
true according to Scripture. We said that the fitness
for heaven ought to be the chief theme of the preachers.
The Scripture also sustains this proposition. Paul declares of his preaching Christ, "Whom we preach,
warning every man, and teaching every man in all wisdom; that we may present every man perfect in Christ
Jesus" (*Col. i.* 28). In *Eph. iv.* 10–13, he uses a beautiful classical allusion. He refers to the custom at the
Roman military triumph, when the proud, victorious
general, leading his captives through the city, showered
gold and silver among the people. The gifts that Jesus
gave men when he arose in his triumph from the grave
were the divers orders of the ministry. "And he gave
some, apostles; and some, prophets; and some, evangel-

ists ; and some, pastors and teachers ; for the perfecting of the saints, for the work of the ministry, for the edifying of the body of Christ."

So we see this is the especial work of the ministry, and should be their theme, their specialty. Any preaching that is not to tell the people what it is, or how to get it, or how to keep it, and how to help others to get it, is off the track, and is doing the people a cruel wrong. Describing a scene of nature, painting the beauties of nature, dealing in pathetic narratives, diving into the bowels of the earth to describe the wonders of geology, scraping the stars to tell about astronomy, disquisitions upon science, rhetoric, physical culture, etc., may display the attainments of the preacher ; but it is not the preaching to which Christ has called his ministers.

How astonishing that the ministry ever allow themselves to treat gingerly, or not at all, the very theme which the Lord sent them to preach. Let us see if our third proposition is sustained by Scripture, which was, holiness ought to be the specialty of everybody. The Bible also teaches this in harmony with common sense. In *Deut. vi.* 5, God says to Israel, " And thou shall love the Lord thy God with all thine heart, and with all thy soul, and with all thy might. And these words, which I command thee this day, shalt be in thine heart : and thou shalt teach them diligently unto thy children, and shalt talk of them when thou sittest in thine house, and when thou walkest by the way and when thou liest down, and when thou risest up. And thou shalt bind them for a sign upon thine hand, and they shall be as frontlets between thine eyes." This was

making a specialty of holiness indeed, — breakfast, din-
ner, supper, — all the time.   Again Paul says, " Take
heed, brethren, lest there be in any of you an evil heart
of unbelief, in departing from the living God.   But exhort one another daily, while it is called to-day ; lest
any of you be hardened through the deceitfulness of
sin."   It will be seen that he exhorts us to give daily
exhortations to the brethren to holiness of heart.   This
is making holiness a specialty indeed.   It is the specialty of heaven, and ought to be on earth.   In the good
time coming, Zechariah says it will be written on the
bells of the horses.   It will be a specialty then *sure*, and
there is no reason why it should not be now.

Proposition four is also thoroughly Scriptural : It
ought to be possessed every moment is the teaching of
the Word of God.   In the parable of the Lord and his
watching servants, Jesus said, " Therefore be ye also
ready."   He did not say get ready, for the man who
has to get ready is not ready.   He expects us to be in
a state of readiness all the time.   There is a fallacious
teaching abroad that there are two kinds of grace, — one
called "living grace," and another called "dying grace."
It is a mistake ; there is but one kind — living grace.
If we have that it will take us *through*.   No man is fit
to live until he has the grace that makes him ready to
die any moment.   What a vast amount of self-deception
there is among church-members who know they are not
fit for heaven, but hope to get there sometime, some-
how.   If the summons should reach you, reader, that at
midnight you would be obliged to change worlds, and
you had to get ready to meet God, it shows that you are
not now ready.   People who are ready do not need to

get ready. People who have to get ready are not ready. Any man to whom "sudden death would not be sudden glory " has no salvation worth having. How will it be with the man called suddenly, who was expecting to grow into holiness. Brother, if you should die in one of your fits of temper, where would you go to ?

The proposition that the fitness for heaven must be within the reach of all classes, high and low, is also taught in the Bible. Some people have thought that holiness was only for the apostles or preachers, and evangelists. But Isaiah sets the matter right. In chapter xxxv. he speaks of the way of holiness, and says, " The wayfaring men, though fools, shall not err therein." No one who knows enough to make an excuse can possibly offer this excuse.

Peter, too, says on the day of Pentecost, " For the promise is unto you, and to your children, and to all that are afar off, even as many as the Lord our God shall call." And Jesus, after having prayed for his disciples, that they might be sanctified, said, " Neither pray I for these alone, but for them also which shall believe on me through their word." We asserted in our sixth proposition that whatever was essential to fit us for heaven ought to be found sufficient to qualify us for all of life's duties ; because if the ministry had to preach one Sunday on one sin and another on another, it would take a whole lifetime to get around. We need to have a controlling power that would enable us to do right at once. Does the Bible speak of any such fitness ? It does. Solomon says, " Keep thy heart with all diligence, for out of it are the issues of life." Here, then, we have the essential for heaven, — " Holiness, without which no man shall see the Lord." We knew a pastor several years ago who preached on this text. It caused quite a stir among the people. One man commenced the next day to canvass the parish to make complaints of the sermon. He came to one person with these words. " Our preacher said something awful yesterday." "What was it?" was the inquiry. " He said that no one could get to heaven without holiness." " No, you are mistaken," was the rejoinder. "What did he say then?" " It was not he that said it, but the Lord," was the reply.

Yes, God says it. And yet many are trying to get to heaven without it. As a leading evangelist says, " Morality will keep us out of jail, but it will take holiness to keep us out of hell." It was to make men holy, to lead them right on to holiness, that God converted us. This is the objective point of our being called out of the world, to assume the name and life of Christians. Just as God led Israel out of Egypt in order to lead them into Canaan, so he leads us out of the world to lead us into the experience of entire sanctification.

CHAPTER XII.

HOLY FIRE.

"He is like a refiner's fire." — MAL. iii. 2.

THE ancient Greeks in their mythology tell us that Prometheus stole fire from heaven to give life to a man whom he had fashioned. For this he was most severely and eternally punished. It was a mistaken idea, that fire had to be stolen from heaven. God is more than willing that we should have heavenly fire. He has fashioned the heart of man to be the place where fire may glow unceasingly. Under the Old Testament economy God taught spiritual truths by symbols. He had to use the kindergarten method, illustrating spiritual truths by material things. "Which is a parable for the time now present" (*R. V.*), says the apostle, in speaking of the Old Testament economy. This method is necessary because man is slow to perceive spiritual things.

God uses several symbols to represent the work of the Holy Spirit. Fire, water, wind, and oil are the four symbols usually employed to represent the office and work of the Holy Spirit. From the earliest time fire has been the most common symbol of the presence of God among men. It is believed that when Abel received the testimony that his offering was accepted, it was by fire falling upon his sacrifice. When Abraham had offered

his sacrifice, dividing the pieces of the slain victims,
then the smoking furnace and the burning lamp passed
between the pieces, denoting that God was present to
accept his sacrifice.   When the tabernacle was erected,
and the sacrifice had been placed upon the altar, "There
came a fire out from before the Lord, and consumed
upon the altar the burnt offering and the fat."   When
Solomon had ceased his prayer at the dedication of the
temple, then fire fell from heaven upon the sacrifice.
Elijah received the answer from heaven by fire, in his
contest with the prophets of Baal.   The answer came
from "the God that answereth by fire."   The glory of
the first temple was the fire that had thus fallen from
heaven, and was ever kept burning.   When the second
temple was dedicated, no fire fell on the altar ; and yet
it was said of that second temple, "the glory of this
latter house shall be greater than that of the former."
That greater glory consisted in the fact that Jesus
Christ himself, in the flesh, walked and taught in the
temple.   And when Jesus yielded up his life, and the
veil of the temple was rent in twain, and the old dispensation had passed away, then the Holy Spirit fell
upon that company in the upper room, and tongues of
fire rested upon their heads.   This was the last time
the symbol of fire appeared.   All down through the
ages it had been leading to this event.   The real fire
had appeared in the hearts of men.   The symbol henceforth was no more.   It was no longer needed.   Now
the believer may receive the real fire, glowing, never
dying.   This takes place in the blessing of entire sanctification.   When John the Baptist came, baptizing with
water, as an emblem or symbol of regeneration, he de-

clared of the coming of Christ: "He shall baptize you with the Holy Ghost, and with fire," referring to the fact that when Jesus returned to heaven, he would send the Holy Spirit to dwell in the hearts of those who desired him, as an abiding presence. Some have misunderstood the term fire in this passage to refer to a third blessing, called the baptism with fire. Nothing could do more violence to the interpretation of the Scriptures. Water is the symbol of regeneration usually. Fire is always the symbol of the sanctifying work of the Spirit. For this reason John, who was preaching, "He that believeth on the Son hath everlasting life," baptized those who received this "everlasting life" as a token that they had received what Paul subsequently calls "the washing of regeneration." To use this faulty interpretation in other places would be ridiculous. For instance, Jesus said to Nicodemus, "Except a man be born of water and of the Spirit, he cannot enter into the kingdom of God." He could not have meant another birth by water after he had been born of the Spirit, but simply that the operation of the Spirit in the new birth is symbolized by water. The baptism with water was the beautiful symbol of the washing away of the old life by the Holy Spirit in the new birth. So, when John declared that Jesus should baptize with the Holy Ghost and fire, he declared not two baptisms, but *the* one baptism of the Holy Ghost, of whose administration in the heart fire was the symbol. And just as John made water the symbol as he "gave the knowledge of salvation unto his people, by the remission of their sins" (*Luke i. 77*), so Jesus gave the symbol of the tongue of fire resting upon the heads of the disciples, as he baptized them with the Holy Ghost, "purifying their hearts by faith." Therefore we understand by fire the nature and process of the experience wrought in the heart by the Holy Spirit in entire sanctification. The symbol enables us the better to understand what the Holy Spirit does in entire sanctification. It helps us to better comprehend the work accomplished. Let us notice some of the uses and operations of fire. This will help us the better to discover the different results accomplished by the Spirit when he comes into the heart in his fulness.

I. *Fire penetrates.*

When any metal, no matter how hard or impenetrable to other forces, is thrown into the fire, it is penetrated through and through by the fire. Every part is reached by it. Water and air cannot go where the fire is. It works internally. So does the Holy Spirit. His chief work is within, where no human eye can see his working. True religion is mostly an inside affair. While its manifestations may be seen to some extent on the outside, yet the chief work is within. This was the point where the Pharisees made their great and fatal mistake. Jesus said to them, "Ye Pharisees make clean the outside of the cup and the platter; but your inward part is full of ravening and wickedness. Ye fools, did not he that made that which is without make that which is within also?" There is an amazing amount of modern Phariseeism that does not recognize the same fact that God made the inner man as well as the outer man. A great multitude of modern religionists are garnishing the outer man, and paying little or no attention to heart religion. And when much is said about the latter, it is called "mysticism" or "fanaticism," etc. There never was a time when we needed to contend more for the inward religion, made possible and actual by the indwelling Holy Spirit. Jesus declared to the disciples, "He dwelleth with you and shall be in you." This is spiritual religion indeed. A great mass of professed Christians know nothing of it, by their own admission. It becomes a great question, How shall we get men to see that this is an internal religion? People say, "If there is anything wrong in my heart, I want it removed." But if we let the Holy Spirit come in, he will search all the wrong out and discover it.

Let him come in and have his way, and it will be unnecessary to imply the doubt by saying, "if there is is anything wrong," for —

II. *Fire purifies.*

Malachi says of the Holy Spirit, "He shall sit as a refiner and purifier of silver." Only the most intense heat will separate the dross from the pure metal. Water will cleanse the outside of the precious ore, removing dirt, gravel, clay, etc. Hence the symbol of water in describing the work of the Spirit in the new birth. Regeneration makes a clean outside life. But fire is an agent for internal cleansing. Only holy fire will burn sin out of the heart. Men have tried penance and zeal; but these only harden, while they do not purify. They feed the self-life and increase pride. Only the fire of the Holy Ghost will kill out the demons of lust and pride. Inbred sin is hell-fire in the soul. And there is only one fire that is hotter, that will burn out the dross and leave the pure gold only.

III. *Fire transforms.*

It penetrates and heats until the substance put into it becomes all on fire itself. It makes things wholly given to it like itself. We think this is what the apostle means when he says we "are changed into the same image from glory to glory, even as by the Spirit of the Lord." God is love; and the complete possession of the soul by the spirit of God permeates it through and through, until it is dissolved in love. We may be transformed before we are translated; and, in fact, unless we are transformed, we shall never be translated.

IV. *Fire melts.*

The fierce heat of the sun unlocks the icy fetters of spring, causes the ice to dissolve, and makes the rivers overflow. Nothing is more needed to-day in modern Christianity than something to melt the frozen performances called religion. We have gone to the extreme in the pursuit of the intellectual, and have stifled the emotions. Man needs a religion to enlarge and set on fire his emotional nature. The devil is getting too great a hold on the affectional nature of man, which many of the pulpits have been starving, until it has come to be thought that joy and peace are more to be found in the service of the devil than the service of God. We hear many tell of "serving God on principle." But it should be the principle of love. He who does not serve him from love makes him a taskmaster.

> Holy fire melts the heart,
> Makes the ills of life depart.

V. *Fire melts in order to mould.*

When metals by means of heat are reduced to the

flux state, they can be run into any mould, and fashioned into whatever shape we please. And so, when the holy fire melts the heart, it becomes pliable. There are so many stubborn, stiff-necked people, whose obstinacy and pride are unbending. But the melting fire cures this. They become humble and docile, ready to be moulded as God desires. For purity is not only to fit us for heaven, but make us useful here. The gold and silver are melted and purified, only to be made into something useful for the service of man. And God has purified us to make us each "a vessel unto honor, sanctified, and meet for the master's use, and prepared unto every good work." (2 *Tim. ii.* 21.) Our holiness means service to both God and man. We are not sanctified for our own happiness alone, but for service.

VI. *Fire shines.*

This is the principle by which we light our dwellings and streets. A fire is the cause of the shining. Holy fi.e, too, puts a shine on our actions, words, yea, even our faces. Men of old who had been into the presence of God had shining faces. Moses had to put a veil on his face when he came down from the presence of God, because his face shone so that the children of Israel could not look upon it. Stephen's face caught the glory of God before he died, for he was "full of the Holy Ghost." The supernatural fire within irradiates the natural sometimes. We remember, on one occasion, at a great meeting where God was baptizing his people with holy fire, that a little boy said to his mother, "See these people's faces, mother; they look as if they were lit up with the electric light." There has been too much long-faced religion. People not saved from sin

get wrinkled and care-worn very early in life through
fret and worry. We have seen many a placid face
whose look reminded us of the way the Sea of Galilee
must have looked after the voice of Jesus hushed it to
a calm. Inquiring into the cause, we have learned that
it was the reflection of holy fire within. This is better
than cosmetics or face-powders. Jesus said of John
the Baptist, "He was a burning and a shining light."
He had to burn before he could shine. So must we
burn first, then we will shine. If people had this internal fire they would not need, nor care so much, to em-
bellish the outside.

VII. *Fire is attractive.*

It catches the eye. It lights up the gloom of the
night. A house on fire will attract a crowd. When we
were a boy we sometimes ran for miles to see a fire.
When we go into a room with a fire in the open fire-
place, it constantly attracts the eye. This is the divine
method of attracting men to the gospel. What hard
work some churches have to draw a crowd, — sensational
themes, artistic music, eloquent oratory, etc. But the
divine method is to set the church on fire, and the com-
munity will come out to see it burn. He set the
church at Jerusalem on fire ; and the whole city turned
out, and three thousand were converted. When God
sets a pulpit on fire by baptizing the preacher, he never
lacks an audience. Is it not strange that any pulpit
should have every thing else in the place of fire ?

VIII. *Fire is the great source of motion.*

All the great methods of transportation to-day depend upon fire as their source. The locomotive is useless without fire. The dynamo generates no electricity

without fire as its source of motion. This causes the difference between steam and sailing vessels. The latter make no progress except when the wind blows, while the former go against wind and tide. There seem to be two kinds of Christians : one who goes well when everything is favorable, and the other who goes against the waves and storms of opposition and trial because they have holy fire within. We like the term "holiness movement" given to the present revival of holiness, because it *moves*, and makes things *move* wherever it goes. Dead professors, moribund churches, and dying camp-meetings are revived and invigorated by it. There is the swing of conquest in it. When the holy fire possesses a soul, it gives him ceaseless energy. Perpetual motion has been discovered at last. It is in a fire-baptized soul. No wonder such people are irrepressible. No wonder the holiness movement keeps moving, notwithstanding there is so much opposition. Notwithstanding there are so few workers to help it, yet it goes right on. We have sometimes thought of the homely illustration of the housekeeper, who puts the clothes in the boiler. After a while she presses down the part that boils up, but it is only to have them rise up in another place. So men have thought that holiness was crowded down and under, but it springs up in another place. The reason of it is, *there is fire underneath*. John the Baptist is beheaded, but Jesus comes. He is crucified; but the holy fire falls on the church he has left behind him, until enemies cry, "These that have turned the world upside down are come hither also." It cannot be quenched, for holy fire is in it.

IX. *Everything is useless without fire.*

Let the fire of the sun go out for one day, and all life would fail from this earth. Fuel is useless without fire. The coal in the mines of the earth is valueless, except as it can be put in contact with fire. How much talent there is in the church wasting to-day, that amounts to nothing because it has never been touched with fire. How many people who never have amounted to anything because they did not get the fire. We have seen men of very moderate talents accomplish great things for God and humanity, and die lamented, while those of great talent accomplished nothing. It is a sad fact that most people never amount to any-thing. Sometimes God takes an uncultured man, who violates the rules of grammar, and murders the king's English, and makes him a power to shame those of education and talent, who are trusting in their culture instead of the Holy Ghost. Let us remember that un-less we get the fire we never shall amount to anything. With it we can be useful.

X. *We can endure most anything if we get fire enough.*

Elijah on Mt. Carmel turned twelve barrels of water over his sacrifice ; but when the fire came from heaven it consumed everything, and licked up the water. Holy fire will destroy all that would depress or quench our spirits. There will be plenty of people to throw cold water if we attempt to serve God ; but if we only get fire enough it will save us from all discouragement, and keep us in the midst of every trial. We pity those people who are constantly telling about their trials and persecutions. The trouble is they have not got the fire.

Some people talk about leaving the church because they are opposed. What they need is the fire which will enable them to endure hardness with joyfulness.

XI. *Holy fire will not destroy anything worth keeping.*

There are people who do much questioning as to what the Lord will do or will not do for them in sanctifying their souls. They almost seem afraid that something will be destroyed that will injure their character. Some years ago we heard the matter illustrated by the burning bush that Moses saw on the mount. The bush was all on fire, yet not consumed. But if there had been a last year's bird's nest, a hornet's nest, or a spider's web, they would have been destroyed. If we have a heart where the devil hatches out evil thoughts and tempers, the fire will not destroy our heart, but will burn up all that which is unclean. If we have a hornet's nest that sends out spiteful, stinging words that hurt others all about us, holy fire will destroy these evil things without destroying us. Sin has made mankind unnatural. Holy fire takes out the abnormal element of sin, and makes us natural. Far from injuring us, it makes us better. We shall retain all worth keeping, and lose everything else. When people really get hungry for holiness, they will not be quibbling as to being hurt, or what they will have to lose to obtain it.

XII. *Fire sets fire.*

It may be only a spark, but it has to be *real fire* to start a fire. And a very small spark is enough to burn up a great city. " Behold, how great a matter a little fire kindleth," says St. James. Samson's foxes did great havoc in the conflagration that destroyed the

corn of the Philistines. It was not the foxes that made
the great fire that overspread the country, but it was
the firebrand that Samson tied to the tips of their
tails. It is not great talents that God blesses so much
as ordinary talents set on fire. You may not have
strength or capacity to carry more than a spark; but
if it be real fire that you carry, God will set some one
else on fire. Let us, then, remember that we have no
excuse for not carrying all the fire of which our capacity will admit. We have seen whole churches aflame
because some humble member got a spark of real Jerusalem fire.

XIII. *Fire never falls upon an empty altar.*

It was when the sacrifice was all upon the altar at
the dedication of the tabernacle that the fire fell. It
was so likewise when Solomon dedicated the temple.
Then the fire fell. It never falls until the sacrifice is
fully put there. So was it on the day of Pentecost.
Reader, if the fire has not yet fallen upon the altar of
your heart, depend upon it, you are yet keeping back
part of the price. If you do not know what you are
keeping back, would you be willing to pray, " Lord,
show me what it is, and it shall go upon the altar, no
matter what it may be " ? Put all upon the altar, to
stay forever! " Bind the sacrifice with cords, even
unto the horns of the altar," says the Psalmist. He
means, put it there to stay, as an everlasting covenant.
And when it is all thus placed, depend upon it, fire
will fall upon it from heaven. You are the sacrifice.
God wants you wholly given up to him.

XIV. *An altar is of no use without fire.*

That is the purpose of an altar. Alas! there are

so-called altars without fire. They have painted resem-
blances of fire, but no fire. Painted fire consumes
nothing, and gives no heat. There are many such
heartless performances in the name of the religion of
Jesus Christ. There is much ministering at cold altars
by shivering priests. There is much ridicule to-day of
the altar that has the fire ; but that is the only purpose
of an altar, to receive and keep fire. That is the only
reason God made the heart, — that it might glow with
celestial fire. We might as well have no altars if we
are to have only false, painted fires, — imitations that
consume nothing, and give no heat. All the heat the
priest got in the tabernacle was from the altar-fires.
Many people are told to " believe, believe ;" but they do
not hold on until they get the fire, and then they go
away and give way to unholy tempers. What is the
trouble ? They do not hold on in faith until they get
the fire that consumes sin. Of what use to have religion, unless we get the fire. If we are going to have
anything to do with the religion of Jesus Christ, let us
have all there is in it. It is of no use to have a professed altar without *real fire*.

XV. *Everything worth having comes after we get the
fire.*

The disposition in the modern church is to put everything else in the foreground — elegance, wealth, culture, numbers, etc. But if we would prosper according
to the divine idea of prosperity, we must have the fire
first, and then everything else worth having will follow.
Elijah was petitioned by Ahab to bring about a ces-
sation of the drought. Ahab wanted the rain. But
Elijah prayed first for and received the fire, then pray-

ing for the rain was successful. A great many churches
and ministers want rain, without fire. They see the
need of rain ; the country is very dry spiritually ; they
see things are drying up. They want the rain, but
dread the fire. As a last resort they send for some
Elijah who can bring down fire, that rain may follow,
and the cause be helped. Let all God's people be
Elijahs, with no backslidden Ahabs, and there will be
no drought and plenty of fire. Let all dead Christians
and churches get the fire, and there will be plenty of
everything else needful.

XVI. *Fire is terrible when we get in the wrong relation to it.*

The most useful of servants, fire becomes a terrible
enemy when we get into wrong relations to it. Holy
fire is "a savor of life unto life, or of death unto death."
"Our God is a consuming fire." He will either consume sin, or he will consume us. Each of us has the
alternative either to be purified or destroyed. We have
tried to show the reader the blessed results that come
from the reception of the baptism with the Holy Ghost.
We trust God will by these feeble words stimulate our
readers to seek to become true Christians, and not to
rest short of obtaining the holy fire, which God is
anxious to bestow on those who will get to the place
where the fire falls.

> " Now I feel the sacred fire,
> Kindling, flaming, glowing,
> Higher still and rising higher,
> All my soul o'erflowing."

www.ingramcontent.com/pod-product-compliance
Lightning Source LLC
Chambersburg PA
CBHW032015010726
47493CB00007B/2409